Un

◆

Two Erotic Novellas

Guillaume Apollinaire

FLESH UNLIMITED
Guillaume Apollinaire
ISBN 1 871592 56 9
Velvet 4
A compendium edition of
Les Onze Mille Verges
&
Les Mémoires D'Un Jeune Don Juan
Translated by
Alexis Lykiard
Copyright © Alexis Lykiard 1995
This edition
Copyright © Creation Books 1995
All rights reserved
Published by
CREATION BOOKS
83 Clerkenwell Road
London EC1, UK
Tel: 0171-430-9878
Fax: 0171-242-5527

Design: Bradley Davis
Cover photograph: Matthew Gardner
Model: Louiza
A Butcherbest Production

Flesh
Unlimited

♦

INTRODUCTION

In 1935 the gifted teenage poet David Gascoyne, referred in *A Short Survey Of Surrealism* to Apollinaire as "a man whose energetic enthusiasm was one of the main driving forces behind the beginnings of... 'the modern movement', a term that is meaningless enough now but that comprised during the few years before the War, Apollinaire's heyday, all the new ideas and styles that have revitalised art in our time... cubism, futurism, dadaism, found in him their staunchest champion... no doubt he would have championed surrealism... had he lived to see it born." In 1995 that remains true, but Gascoyne had also reminded Thirties readers that *surrealist* was an adjective invented by Apollinaire.

Indeed, Guillaume Albert Wladimir Alexandre Apollinaire de Kostrowitzky (1880-1918) was boundlessly influential and inventive, most importantly reinventing *himself* in 1902, with his first publication, as "Guillaume Apollinaire". Born in Rome, illegitimate son of a young beauty from the minor Polish nobility and a much older, rich Catholic Franco-Italian-Swiss army officer, Apollinaire was educated in Monaco and Nice, travelled widely, led a very uncertain and unsettled existence yet turned into one of the great French writers of the twentieth century. He did not become a French national until quite soon before his death, however: when, after fighting for France in both artillery and infantry during World War One, he was badly wounded in the head and then trepanned. He recovered, only to die in the Paris 'flu epidemic of November 1918.

How this cosmopolitan, enigmatic, magnetic personality – belonging chronologically half in the nineteenth century and half in the twentieth – became such a formidable and trailblazing impresario for the creative art-forms and such a fine practitioner and critic of so many of them, has been well and amply detailed elsewhere. (Outside France, Apollinaire has been lucky with his biographers, critics and translators: Francis Steegmuller, Cecily Mackworth, Roger Shattuck, Oliver Bernard, Ron Padgett and others have written engagingly and perceptively about him and translated his poetry and shorter fiction into English.) Perhaps all that should be mentioned here is that Apollinaire was both fully of, and ahead of, his time. As he himself declared: *'Il faut aimer son époque. Notre 20e siècle est bien plus passionnant que le 19e'*, and he was the heir not only of Lautréamont (1846-70) but of Jarry, who died the year these novels were first published. That is to say his lyricism, black humour and erudition, like theirs, combined to express profound dissatisfaction with everything traditionally considered 'picturesque' or 'literary' – academic artifice and bogus realism alike. Original, therefore often disconcerting, structures were needed to express the new modern spirit. For Apollinaire this would mean a constant play with both form and content – via puns, quirky punctuation (or lack of it), neologism, typographical experiment, rapid transitions, and, more generally, the merging of fact and fantasy in inventive verbal collages to parallel what was being achieved in the visual arts by the cubists and his great friend Picasso.

The work of creation, furthermore, means recreation; work is (or should also be) play, serious play where extremes and opposites meet and are reconciled, to combine in new forms. Re-creation too – activity aware of the past but not in awe of it – using, adapting or celebrating what is needed and jettisoning the rest, while a current language evolves: this surely is the force of Pound's injunction to "make it new".

The work of Apollinaire in general has retained its newness, its freshness, because, as André Billy has written, "Apollinaire is first and foremost a great poet". As for what might appropriately be called the coupling of these two very different novels of nearly ninety years ago, we should remember that they are the work of a young man in his twenties, books rapidly written for the money; yet they are not of course the work of any hack, but of an exceptional talent. And Apollinaire needs no apologists – these are exuberant, excessive narratives rich in the comic absurdity and grim humour that informed all his work. In short, while they may still surprise and even shock readers today, they bear the master's stamp. As Beatrice Faust perceptively notes in *Women, Sex And Pornography* (1980): "Pornography lacks a maker's style as well as a maker's name."

That could not be said of either of these books, although *Memoirs Of A Young Don Juan* is clearly the more traditional in form and content. As a novel of a young boy's growing awareness of sex, this *bildungsroman* has considerable gaiety and charm. John Atkins in *Sex In Literature* (1970) calls it "quite a sincere little book" and – discussing the subject of masturbation – adds that here "one of the best descriptions of this discovery is to be found..." Patrick Kearney, in his excellent 1982 survey, *A History Of Erotic Literature,* terms it "a pleasant, rather innocent book... all written up in an easy matter-of-fact way that softens what in less skilful hands would be offensive."

The Eleven Thousand Rods (also first published in 1907 by Jean Fort), is in extraordinary contrast – quite another proposition. As Kearney writes, "a different sort of book entirely, a brilliant fantasy in which all the demons of some insane, Sadeian hell are unleashed at once... the book is in fact so extreme, so deliberately and self-consciously revolting that Apollinaire's purpose was clearly to parody the genre of ultra-sadistic erotic fiction by taking it to its furthest possible limits. And he succeeds admirably: those who approach the book in anything but the spirit in which it was written are understandably appalled. Once the idea behind it becomes apparent, it is less shocking and takes on the qualities of a surrealist farce." As translator I can only concur. The book certainly reads at times like some goonish deconstruction of de Sade, whose work Apollinaire learnedly catalogued and edited, along with much other erotica, for the Bibliothèque Nationale. What Apollinaire called de Sade – *"un des hommes les plus étonnants qui aient jamais paru"* – might here apply to our author himself. For what are we to make of this heady brew with its wildly orgasmic orgies and carnal carnage? Here the fun is undeniably sinister, mingling Rabelaisian exaggeration, arcane scatology, poetry, and erudite references. Apollinaire in an exasperated impatience with any kind of convention mixes genres, making use of *faits-divers* and recent history (such as the 1904-5 Russo-Japanese War), swift transitions (almost cinematic cross-cutting) and all sorts of grotesqueries whose obsessive effect is sometimes more emetic than stimulating.

It's a weird parodic cubism applied to prose, and, like it or not, inimitable. And yet I am reminded of William Burroughs writing to Allen Ginsberg in the early 1950s: "A medium suitable for me does not yet exist, unless I invent it", or: "It's almost like automatic writing produced by a hostile, independent entity who is saying in effect, 'I will write what I please'... only the most extreme material is available to me." Apollinaire's own peculiar dark vision of things, expressed through a harsh macabre humour (itself the paradoxical converse of the pure, singing lyricism of his poetry) has been enormously influential – and it was clearly in evidence by 1907, well before he encountered the inferno of trench warfare. For Robert Desnos writing in 1923 *(De l'érotisme...)*: *"L'oeuvre de Guillaume Apollinaire en érotisme est la plus importante de ces vingt dernières années"*. Desnos, fine poet and himself a remarkable erotic writer, considered this particular novel, along with *Calligrammes,* to be Apollinaire's masterpiece, stressing that *"cette oeuvre est d'une grande importance"*. Picasso stated *Les Onze Mille Verges* was the best book he'd come across – though as a close friend he may have been biased, since a copy of the book exists inscribed by the author with a delightful dedicatory verse acrostic on the artist's name! Louis Aragon, in a preface to the 1930 reissue of the novel thought such judgements somewhat capricious, his praise taking a different tack: *"C'est peut-être le livre d'Apollinaire où l'humour apparaît le plus purement."*

This emphasis on humour I believe to be vital. For pornography is, and of course always needs to be, humourless. And too many people still think Art (invariably with a capital A!) must be serious if indeed it is to be Art; Art too should be Important and thus humourless. These people (theorists, moralists, hypocrites) themselves lack humour; all too often, whether to relish it or protest about it or both, they interest themselves in pornography. (The connections are there to be made!) I am sure such readers will find Apollinaire's subversive, jocular tone – which I have tried to preserve as faithfully as possible – profoundly offensive.

The fact is that most true artists go beyond what is accepted or acceptable 'in their day': Apollinaire wrote for our day as well as his, and André Breton has noted "eroticism's fundamental need for *transgression"*. As George Steiner, a critic not noted for his support of pornography, wrote in his 1972 essay *Night Words,* "where a Diderot, a Crébillon *fils,* a Verlaine, a Swinburne or an Apollinaire write erotica, the result will have some of the qualities which distinguish their more public works." In Apollinaire's case, most of the qualities... But we ought not to be surprised by this.

In 1888, Henry James (a serious artist if ever there was one) wrote about another scandalous and sardonic French writer, Maupassant, that he "would doubtless affirm that where the empire of the sexual sense is concerned, no exaggeration is possible". This is in the circumstances unexpectedly perceptive and applicable with some justice to Apollinaire too. Yet James, who in other respects seems such a typical Victorian, died only a

9

year or so before Apollinaire. He might also have been prophetically referring to Apollinaire with the final words of his essay: "Let us not be alarmed at this prodigy (though prodigies are alarming)... who is at once so licentious and so impeccable, but gird ourselves up with the conviction that another point of view will yield another perfection."

—*Alexis Lykiard*

THE TEXT

To date, Apollinaire has not been honestly represented in the English language in a role he clearly relished – as author of erotic novels. His first such book, *Mirely, Ou Le Petit Trou Pas Cher* (1901), written very early on in his all too brief career, seems to have been irretrievably lost. English versions of *Memoirs Of A Young Don Juan* (*Exploits*, in later editions) and *Les Onze Mille Verges*, both originally published in 1907, were translated respectively by Richard Seaver and Alexander Trocchi and published by Maurice Girodias's Olympia Press, Paris, in 1953. Both translations were – surprisingly – incomplete and full of misprints and all kinds of errors. (That usually estimable writer Trocchi, for example, several times renders *fesser* as *enculer*, while Seaver also makes some equally startling mistakes.) These Olympian adaptations were of course not for sale in the UK or USA... A mediocre and considerably expurgated English edition of *Les Onze Mille Verges* alone was published in the UK in 1976. That oddity deserves passing mention here if only for the remarkable effect achieved. By coy deletions, absurd paraphrases and many inaccuracies, it somehow contrived to be both longwinded and humourlessly prurient – hence utterly false to the original.

Readers of this Creation Books edition will probably not be surprised to learn that both books have been freely available for many years in France where, in mainstream French paperback editions such as *J'ai Lu*, they are accepted as genre classics. Now,

11

for the first time, the two novels at last appear together, newly translated and complete and unexpurgated, in an English-language edition. I am grateful to two other writer-translators, Gertrude Starink and Harry Guest, for some helpful information and suggestions.

—*A.L.*
January, 1995.

One:
The Eleven Thousand Rods
or,
The Loves Of A Hospodar

♦

Chapter One

Bucharest is a beautiful city where East and West seem to intermingle. If you take into account only the geographic site, you are still in Europe; but you are already in Asia, to go by certain local customs, and if you look at the Turks, the Serbs, and other Macedonian races, picturesque specimens of these may be seen in the streets. And yet this is a Latin country: the thoughts of the Roman soldiers who colonised it were no doubt turned towards Rome, at that time the capital of the world and seat of all the civilized refinements. This Western nostalgia was handed down to their descendants: the Romanians dwell constantly upon a city where luxury is natural, life full of joy. But Rome's splendour has decayed, the queen of cities has surrendered her crown to Paris, and it is hardly surprising if, by some atavistic phenomenon, the thoughts of the Romanians are incessantly turned towards Paris, which has so thoroughly supplanted Rome at the apex of the universe!

Just like other Romanians, the handsome Prince Vibescu dreamed of Paris, City of Light, where the women, all beautiful, are all loose too. While he was still at college in Bucharest, he needed only to think of a Parisian woman, about *the* Parisienne, to get an erection and be obliged to toss off slowly, beatifically. Later he had shot his come into numerous cunts and bumholes of

15

charming Romanian women. Yet he felt a powerful urge to have a Parisienne.

Mony Vibescu came from a very wealthy family. His great-grandfather had been a hospodar, the equivalent in rank to a sub-prefect in France. But this status became hereditary and both the grandfather and father of Mony had borne the title of hospodar. Mony Vibescu should likewise have carried this title in honour of his ancestor.

But he had read enough French novels not to give a damn about sub-prefects: 'Come on,' he'd say, 'isn't it ridiculous to call yourself *sub-prefect* because your great-grandfather was one? It's quite grotesque!' And to be less grotesque he had replaced the title of hospodar-sub-prefect by that of prince. 'There,' he exclaimed, 'is a title that may be transferable by heredity. Hospodar is an administrative function, yet it's fair enough that those who've distinguished themselves in the civil service should have the right to bear a title. I'm ennobling myself. Deep down, I'm an ancestor. My children and my grandchildren will thank me for it.'

Prince Vibescu was very friendly with the Serbian vice-consul, Bandi Fornovski, who, so town rumour went, was gladly buggering the charming Mony. One day the prince dressed formally and set off for the Serbian vice-consulate. In the street everyone noticed him and the women stared and said: 'Looks quite the Parisian, doesn't he?'

Indeed, Prince Vibescu used to walk as Bucharest folk believe Parisians walk, that's to say with rapid little footsteps and wriggling his arse. Quite charming! and when a man walks like that in Bucharest, not a woman can resist him, not even the wife of the Prime Minister.

Arriving at the Serbian vice-consulate's doorway, Mony pissed at some length against the house front, then rang the bell. An Albanian clad in a white *fustanella* came to open the door for him. Prince Vibescu climbed swiftly to the first floor. The vice-consul Bandi Fornovski was stark naked in his drawing room. He lay on a luxurious sofa, stiff-pricked; near him was Mira, a swarthy Montenegran who was tickling his bollocks. She too was naked and, since she was leaning forward, her stance made her fine well-fleshed bum stick out, brown and downy, its delicate skin stretching taut as a drum. Between both buttocks ran quite a deep cranny, fringed with brown hairs, and you could see the forbidden hole round as a pastille. Below, extended her two long and scrawny thighs and, as her position forced Mira to spread them, her cunt could be seen, plump, thick, deeply-cleft and shaded by a dense mane, jet-black. She was not bothered by Mony's arrival. On a chaise-longue in another corner, two pretty girls, both broad in the beam, were goosing each other, uttering little lustful 'Ah's!'. Mony quickly divested himself of his clothes, then, cock aloft, fully rigid, he flung himself upon the two masturbatrices, attempting to separate them. But his hands slipped on their damp and gleaming bodies which were coiled about like snakes. Then, seeing they were dribbling with lust, and furious at being unable to be part of it, he began with the flat of his hand to slap the fat white arse nearest him. As that seemed considerably to excite the bearer of this fat butt, he started whacking it for all he was worth, so much so that pain overcame lust, the pretty girl whose pretty white bottom he had turned pink sat up angrily and said:

--- Filthy tart, you prince of pederasts, don't mess us about, we don't want your fat prick. Go and stuff your sugarstick up Mira. Leave us alone to get on with it. Right, Zulmé?

--- Yeah, Toné! replied the other young woman.

The prince brandished his enormous prick, bawling:

--- What, you young bitches, still playing stinkfinger forever with your arses!

Then, seizing one of them, he tried to kiss her on the mouth. It was Toné, a pretty brunette, whose snowy white body was flecked with delectable beauty spots in certain areas, and these enhanced its whiteness; her face was equally white and a mole on her left cheek lent this pleasing girl a piquant expression. Her chest was adorned with two superb tits hard as marble, encircled by blue, and tipped with delicate strawberry pink, the right one prettily stained by a beauty spot stuck there like a fly, a dispatched fly.[1]

Mony Vibescu in laying hold of her had slid his hands beneath her plump arse, so white and full that it resembled a fine melon which might have ripened under the midnight sun. Each buttock seemed to have been carved from a block of flawless Carrara marble, and the rondure of the thighs' descent resembled the columns of a Greek temple. But what a difference! The thighs were warm and the buttocks cold, which is one sign of good health. The spanking had turned them a bit pink, so it might have been said of these thighs that they were made of cream with raspberries stirred in. This vista raised poor Vibescu to the height of excitement. His mouth sucked each of Toné's firm tits in turn or else fixed upon throat or shoulder, leaving lovebites there. His hands firmly grasped that big arse swelling like a hard yet pulpy water melon. He squeezed those regal buttocks and had inserted his index finger into an arsehole of exquisite tightness. His great knob which was getting harder and harder began ramming at the breach of a charming coral-coloured cunt surmounted by a glistening black fleece. She yelled at him in Romanian: 'No, you're not to fuck me!' and at the same time jerked about with her sweet round chubby thighs. The red and inflamed head of Mony's huge tool had already reached that wet redoubt of Toné's. The latter disengaged herself again, but in making that movement let fly a fart, not a vulgar fart, but a fart with a crystalline timbre which provoked her wild spasm of hysterical laughter. Her resistance slackened, her thighs parted and Mony's mighty engine had already buried its head in the redoubt when Zulmé, Toné's friend and frotting-partner, seized Mony's balls roughly and, squeezing them in her little hand, caused him such pain that the smoking tool abandoned its residence, to the great disappointment of trim-waisted Toné, who was starting to stir that big arse of hers.

Zulmé was a blonde whose thick hair cascaded down to her

heels. She was shorter than Toné, but no less slender and graceful. Her eyes were black, dark-ringed. As soon as she'd let go of the prince's balls, he flung himself on her, saying: 'Right you are! you're going to pay for Toné!' Then, seizing on one pretty titty, he began sucking its tip. Zulmé writhed. To make fun of Mony she shifted about and undulated her belly, at whose base danced a delicious, very curly blonde beard. At the same time she raised aloft a pretty cunt which divided a fine plump motte. Between the lips of this rosy cunt quivered a rather long clitoris which attested to her tribadic habits. The prince's prick was vainly striving to penetrate this redoubt. At last he gripped her buttocks and was about to penetrate when Toné, annoyed at having been denied the discharge of the superb dick, began tickling the young man's heels with a peacock feather. He started to laugh and squirm. The peacock feather went on tickling him; from the heels it moved upwards to the thighs, to the anus, to the prick which dwindled rapidly.

The two wretches, Toné and Zulmé, delighted with their pranks, laughed for quite a time, then, red and breathless, returned to their goosing, embracing and tonguing each other in front of the sheepish and astonished prince. Their arses bobbed up and down in time, their minge-hairs intermingled, their teeth clattered together, the satins of their firm and palpitating breasts were reciprocally creased. At last, writhing and groaning with lust, they came in unison, while the prince again began getting a hard-on. But seeing both of them so wearied by their mutual frigging, he turned towards Mira who was still pawing the vice-consul's cock. Vibescu approached softly and getting his fine dibble to glide between Mira's big buttocks, he inserted it into the half-open and humid cunt of the pretty girl who, the moment she felt the knob of the prick penetrate her, gave a jerk of her arse to make the tool's penetration complete. Then she continued her abandoned movements, while with one hand the prince worked her clitoris and with the other tickled her bubs.

19

His see-saw motion inside her tight-clenching cunt seemed to give Mira keen pleasure which she evinced in ecstatic cries. Vibescu's belly was beating against Mira's behind and the coolness of Mira's bum caused in the prince as pleasurable a sensation as his belly's heat gave the young girl. Soon their movements grew livelier, jerkier, the prince thrust himself against Mira who was panting while she flexed her buttocks. The prince bit her on the shoulder and held her that way. She yelled out:

--- Ah! that's good... wait... harder... harder... hey, hey, take me. Give me your load... Give me the lot... ah... oh!... oh!

And in a joint discharge they flopped down and remained for a moment obliterated. Toné and Zulmé entwined on the chaise-longue were watching them and laughing. The Serbian vice-consul had lit a slim cigarette of Oriental tobacco. When Mony was back on his feet again, he said to him:

--- Now, dear prince, it's my turn. I was waiting for you to arrive and what I got was Mira, giving my prick a going over, but I've reserved the full fruits for you. Come here my pretty quim, my dear little bumboy, here! and let me slip you one.

Vibescu looked at him a moment, then, spitting on the prick being presented him by the vice-consul, he proffered these words:

--- I've really had enough of being buggered by you, it's the talk of the town.

But the vice-consul had stood up, stiff-pricked, and picked up a revolver.

He aimed the pistol at the trembling Mony, who offered him his braced backside, stammering:

--- Bandi, my dear Bandi, you know I love you, bugger me, bugger me.

Smiling, Bandi forced his prick into the elastic hole hidden between the buttocks of the prince. Once in, and with the three women watching him, he flung himself about like a madman, cursing:

--- God's s..t! I'm coming, keep your arse tight, my little quean, squeeze, I'm coming. Squeeze your pretty cheeks.

And wild-eyed, his hands clutching the delicate shoulders, he spent. Afterwards Mony washed himself, dressed again and left, saying he would return after dinner. But when he was home he wrote this letter:

My dear Bandi,
I've had enough of being buggered by you, I've had enough of the women of Bucharest, I've had enough of wasting here my fortune – with which I'd be so happy in Paris. In less than two hours I shall have left. I hope to amuse myself enormously there and I'm bidding you farewell.

—Mony, Prince Vibescu,
Hereditary Hospodar.

The prince sealed the letter and wrote another one to his lawyer, requesting him to liquidate all his assets and forward the whole sum to him in Paris as soon as he knew his address.

Mony took all the ready cash he had, about 50,000 francs, and headed for the railway station. He posted his two letters and caught the Orient Express to Paris.

Chapter Two

--- Mademoiselle, no sooner did I set eyes on you than, mad with love, I felt my genital organs drawn towards your sovereign beauty and I found myself hotter than if I'd drunk a glass of raki.

--- Come off it, what next!

--- I lay my fortune and my love at your feet. If I were holding you in a bed, I'd prove my passion for you twenty times over. May the eleven thousand virgins or even eleven thousand rods chastise me if I lie![2]

--- You bet your life!

--- My feelings are not false. I don't talk like this to every woman. I am no rake.

--- Get lost!

This conversation was exchanged on the boulevard Malesherbes one sunny morning. The month of May was making nature reappear, and the Paris sparrows chirped love in the newly greened trees. Gallantly Prince Mony Vibescu was making these remarks to a slim, pretty girl who, elegantly dressed, was going on down towards the Madeleine. He was following her with some difficulty since she walked so quickly. All of a sudden she turned round abruptly and burst out laughing:

--- Quite done, have you; I'm pushed for time just now. I'm going to see a girlfriend in the rue Duphot, but if you're ready to take on two women crazy about love and lust, if in fact you're a man of means and sexual prowess, come with me.

He rose to his full height, exclaiming:

--- I am a Romanian prince, an hereditary hospodar.

--- And I, said she, am Culculine d'Ancône, I'm nineteen, I've already drained the balls of ten men well-versed in the arts of love, plus the purses of fifteen millionaires.

And conversing pleasantly on various frivolous or arousing topics the prince and Culculine reached rue Duphot. They rose via a lift to a first floor.

--- Prince Mony Vibescu... my friend Alexine Mangetout.

The introduction was made very gravely by Culculine in a luxurious boudoir decorated with obscene Japanese engravings.

The two friends kissed, without deploying tongues. They were both tall women but not excessively so.

Culculine was a brunette, her grey eyes sparkled with mischief, and a hirsute beauty spot graced the base of her left cheek. Her complexion was sallow, below its skin her blood coursed, her cheeks and forehead wrinkled readily, attesting to her preoccupation with money and love.

Alexine was blonde, of that hue close to the ash-blonde one sees only in Paris.

Her clear complexion seemed transparent. This pretty girl appeared, in her charming pink négligée, as delicate and as impish as a saucy marquise of the century before last.

The acquaintance was soon effected and Alexine, who had had a Romanian lover, went to look for his photograph in her bedroom. The prince and Culculine followed her in. They both flung themselves on her and undressed her laughingly. Her robe fell off, leaving her in a cambric shift which revealed a charming plump body and dimpled bottom.

Mony and Culculine tumbled her onto the bed and brought to light her beautiful pink breasts, large and hard, whose nipples Mony sucked. Culculine leaned down and, raising the shift, uncovered large rounded thighs that met together beneath a pussy ash-blonde, like her hair. Alexine, emitting little cries of pleasure, drew up her tiny feet back onto the bed, causing her mules to drop with a sharp clatter to the floor. Legs spread wide, she was hoisting her arse to her friend's licking while her hands clasped Mony around the neck.

The result was not long in the achieving, her buttocks tightened, her kicking grew more violent, she discharged, saying:

--- Bastards, you're exciting me, you must satisfy me.

--- He promised to do it twenty times! said Culculine, and she undressed.

The prince did likewise. They were naked at the same time, and while Alexine lay swooning on the bed, they were able to admire each other's bodies. Culculine's fleshy arse was swaying deliciously beneath a very narrow waist and Mony's big balls were swollen below an enormous prick of which she grabbed hold.

--- Put it in her, she said. You can do me after.

The prince brought his member up to Alexine's half-open cunt which quivered at this approach:

--- You're killing me! she cried out.

But the prick penetrated to the very balls and withdrew to re-enter like a piston. Culculine clambered onto the bed and rested her black pussy at Alexine's mouth, while Mony licked her bum-hole. Alexine was wriggling her arse like a lunatic, she stuck one finger in the arsehole of Mony whose cock got still stiffer with this caress. He brought his hands back under Alexine's buttocks which tensed with an incredible force, gripping inside her burning cunt the enormous prick which could hardly move in there.

Soon the commotion of the three characters was extreme, their breathing turned into gasps. Alexine came thrice, then it was the turn of Culculine who immediately moved down so as to nibble Mony's balls. Alexine began yelling like one damned and writhed like a snake when Mony fired off into her snatch his Romanian fuck. At once Culculine jerked him out of the hole and her mouth replaced the prick to lap up the sperm leaking out in large

25

dollops. Alexine, meanwhile, had taken in her mouth Mony's prick which she well and truly cleaned, thereby giving him a renewed hard-on.

A moment later the prince hurled himself on Culculine, but his prick remained at the portal tickling the clitoris. He held in his mouth one of the young woman's tits. Alexine was caressing them both.

--- Put it in me, Culculine cried, I can't bear it any longer.

But the prick was still outside. She came twice and seemed desperate when the prick abruptly pierced her up to the uterus, then wild with excitement and lust she bit Mony so hard on the ear that a piece of it lodged in her mouth. She swallowed it, screaming at full throttle and bucking her bum imperiously. This wound from which the blood was flowing in gouts seemed to excite Mony, for he began thrusting more vigorously and did not quit Culculine's quim till he had discharged a total of three times and she herself ten.

When he had decunted, both noticed in astonishment that Alexine had disappeared. She soon returned with pharmaceutical products for bandaging Mony and an enormous coachman's whip.

--- I bought it for fifty francs, she exclaimed, from the cabby of Hackney 3269, and it's going to help us give the Romanian another stand. Let him dress his ear, Culculine darling, and we'll do 69 to get ourselves excited.

While he was staunching his blood, Mony watched this exhilarating spectacle: top to tail, Culculine and Alexine gamahuched each other with gusto. Alexine's large arse, white and chubby-cheeked, was waddling over Culculine's face; their tongues, long as childpricks, worked on steadily, saliva and come combined, the sodden short-hairs plastered together and sighs, heart-rending had they not been sighs of lust, rose from the bed which creaked and groaned under the pleasant weight of the pretty girls.

--- Come and bugger me! cried Alexine.

But Mony was losing so much blood that he no longer wanted a horn. Alexine stood up and, grabbing the whip of cabby 3269, a superb brand new stock at that, brandished it and lashed the back and buttocks of Mony, who, under this new pain, began to yell. But Alexine, naked and akin to a maniacal maenad, went on whipping him.

--- Come and spank me too!, she cried to Culculine, whose eyes were flashing and who started to thrash Alexine's big, bobbing arse for all she was worth. Culculine was soon excited too.

--- Spank me, Mony! she pleaded, and he, becoming used to the punishment, although his body was bleeding, began to slap the fine dusky buttocks which opened and closed rhythmically. When he'd developed a hard-on, the blood was flowing not just from his ear but also from each wheal left by the cruel whip.

Alexine turned round then and proffered her prettily roseate rear to the enormous prick which penetrated her rosebud, while she, impaled, cried out and shook arse and tits about. But Culculine, laughing, separated them. The two women resumed their gamahuching while Mony, bleeding all over, and again up to the hilt in Alexine's arse, thrust with a vigour that gave his partner excruciating spasms of pleasure. His balls like the bells of Notre-Dame swung back and forth and dangled against Culculine's nose. There was one moment when Alexine's arsehole squeezed with great force round the root of Mony's rod so he could no longer shunt. It was thus he discharged in long jets sucked from him by the avid anus of Alexine Mangetout.

Meanwhile in the street a crowd had mustered around cab 3269 whose coachman had no whip.

A policeman asked him what he had done with it.

--- I sold it to a lady in the rue Duphot.

--- Go and buy it back or I'll bloody book you.

--- I'm on my way, said the Jehu,[3] a Norman of unusual strength, and after getting directions from the concierge, he rang the first floor bell.

Alexine opened the door for him starkers; at this the coachman had a brain-storm and, as she fled into the bedroom, he dashed after her, pinioned her and slipped a respectably-proportioned prick into her from the rear. Soon he ejaculated, shouting: 'Well I'm damned, God's brothel, fucking slut!'

Alexine with a few strokes of her arse came at the same time, while Mony and Culculine were convulsed with laughter. The coachman, thinking they were making fun of him, flew into a terrible rage.

--- Ah! whores, pimp, carrion, dung, cholera, so you're making a fool of me! My whip, where's my whip?

And catching sight and hold of it, he laid about him with all his might at Mony, Culculine and Alexine, whose naked bodies leapt about under the lashes that left bloody welts. Then he began getting another hard-on and, jumping upon Mony, started to bugger him.

The front door had remained open and the copper, not seeing the coachman return, had gone up and at that moment entered the bedroom; it didn't take him long to produce his regulation prick. This he introduced into the arse of Culculine who clucked like a hen and shivered at the cold contact of the uniform buttons.

Alexine, then unoccupied, took the white baton which was dangling in the sheath at the policeman's side. She inserted it into her cunt and soon these five individuals began shagging all over the place, while the blood from the wounds ran onto the carpets, the sheets and the furniture and while in the street the abandoned carriage 3269 was being led off to the pound, its horse letting off the whole way down the street which it perfumed in nauseating fashion.

Chapter Three

Several days after the performance which cabby 3269 and the policeman had completed in so bizarre a fashion, Prince Vibescu had barely recovered from his emotional upheavals. The marks from the flagellation were healed and he was lethargically stretched out on a sofa in a drawing-room of the Grand Hotel. To stimulate himself he was reading the assorted news items from *Le Journal*. One story fascinated him. The crime was ghastly. A restaurant dishwasher had roasted the rump of a young scullion, then buggered it piping hot and bloodily raw, while eating the best-done bits which came away from the ephebe's posterior. On hearing the howls of the fledgling Vatel[4], the neighbours ran in and the sadistic dishwasher was arrested. The story was recounted in all its details and the prince savoured it while gently tossing off the tool he had pulled out.

Just then, someone knocked. An affable chambermaid, fresh and very pretty in her bonnet and apron, entered at the prince's bidding. She was bearing a letter and blushed on seeing Mony's slipshod condition. He did up his trousers:

--- Don't go away, pretty blonde miss, I need a brief word with you.

At the same time he closed the door and, seizing the pretty Mariette round the waist, kissed her greedily on the mouth. At first she fought him, pursing her lips very tightly, but soon, under the

29

pressure, she began to relax, then her mouth opened. The prince's tongue penetrating inside was at once nipped by Mariette whose mobile tongue itself started tickling the tip of Mony's.

With one hand the young man encircled her waist, with the other he raised her skirts. She wore no drawers. His hand was soon between two fat round thighs one would never guess she had, since she was tall and thin. She had a very hairy cunt. She was very highly-sexed and the hand was soon inside a wet gash, while Mariette was abandoning herself, thrusting her belly forward. Her own hand wandered over Mony's flies, which she managed to unbutton. Thence she tugged out the superb bush-beater she had only glimpsed when entering the room. They frigged each other gently; he diddling her clitoris; she pressing her thumb on his member's meatus. He pushed her onto the sofa where she fell in a sitting position. He lifted her legs and hoisted them onto his shoulders, while she unhooked herself to allow two fine erect tits to pop out. These he began to suck in turn while ramming his hot piledriver into her cunt. Soon she started crying out:

--- That's good, that's so good... ah you do it so well...

Then she bucked her arse in violent spasms and he felt her come as she was saying:

--- Now... I'm coming... now... take it all.

Immediately afterwards, she caught hold of his cock roughly and said:

--- Enough for here.

She pulled it out of her cunt and inserted it into another, absolutely round, hole situated a bit lower down, like a Cyclops eye between two cool white fleshy globes. The prick, lubricated by the feminine spend, penetrated easily and, after buggering vigorously, the prince left his whole load in the arse of the pretty chambermaid. Then he withdrew his cock, which went 'plop' as when one uncorks a bottle, and on its tip there was still some spunk mixed with a bit of shit. At that moment, someone rang from down the corridor and Mariette said: 'I must go and see.' And she dashed off after kissing Mony who pressed two louis into her hand. As soon as she had left, he washed his weapon, then cut open the letter which ran as follows:

My handsome Romanian,
What's become of you? You must have recovered from your exertions. But remember what you told me: If I don't make love twenty times in succession, may eleven thousand rods chastise me. You didn't do it twenty times, so much the worse for you.
The other day you were received in Alexine's dump, rue Duphot. But now we're acquainted you can come to my house. Alexine's is impossible. She can't even receive me. That's why she has her dump. Her senator is too jealous. I don't give a damn myself; my lover's an explorer, he's busy whiling away his time stringing beads with negresses on the Ivory Coast. You can come to my place, 214, rue de Prony. We're expecting you at four o'clock.
—Culculine d'Ancône

As soon as he had read this letter the prince looked at the clock. It was eleven a.m. He rang to summon the masseur, who massaged him and buggered him well and truly. This session revived him. He had a bath and was feeling hale and hearty as he rang for the hairdresser, who dressed his hair and buggered him artistically. The manicurist-pedicurist came up next. He buffed his nails and buggered him vigorously. Then the prince felt absolutely at ease. He went down along the boulevards, had a heavy lunch, then hailed a carriage to take him to the rue de Prony. It was a small residence, and Culculine had the whole of it. An old maidservant showed him in. This place was furnished with exquisite taste.

He was at once led into a bedroom whose brass bed was very low and very wide. The parquet flooring was covered with animal hides which muffled the sound of footsteps. The prince undressed quickly and was stark naked when Alexine and Culculine came in

31

clad in ravishing négligées. They started laughing and kissed him. He began by sitting down, then took the two young women, one on each knee, but raising their skirts so they would remain decently attired and he might feel their bare bums on his thighs. Then he set to frigging them, one for each hand, while they were tickling his prick. When he felt they were well warmed up, he said to them:

--- Now we're going to have a lesson.

He made them sit on a seat facing him and after a moment's reflection said to them:

--- Mesdemoiselles, I have just felt that you are not wearing drawers. You should be ashamed of yourselves. Look sharp and put them on.

When they returned, he began the lesson.

--- Mademoiselle Alexine Mangetout, what is the name of the King of Italy?

--- Think I could care less? said Alexine, I've no idea.

--- Go and get on the bed, cried the teacher.

He made her kneel on the bed with her back turned, then lift her skirts and part the slit in her drawers, whence emerged the gleaming white globes of her buttocks. Then he began slapping her bottom with the flat of his hand; soon the posterior started turning red. This was exciting Alexine who had a fine arse on her, but soon the prince could no longer contain himself. Slipping his hands round the young woman's bust, he grasped her tits beneath the gown then, moving a hand down he tickled her clitoris and felt that her cunt was all wet.

Her own hands had not been inactive; they had seized the prince's prick and directed it into the narrow strait of Sodom. Alexine bent forward to make her arse stick out better and facilitate the entry of Mony's root.

Soon the glans was inside, the rest followed and the balls came to beat against the base of the young woman's buttocks. Culculine, getting fed up, also climbed onto the bed and took to licking the cunt of Alexine who, pleasured both ways, was sobbing with joy. Her body wracked with lust was thrashing about as if she were in agony. Voluptuous whimpers escaped from her wheezing throat. The thick prick filled her arsehole and went back and forth bumping at the membrane that separated it from Culculine's tongue which lapped the juice produced by this pastime. Mony's belly was pounding against Alexine's arse. Soon the prince buggered more vigorously. He began biting the young woman's neck. The tool swelled. Alexine could no longer bear such pleasure; she sank down on top of Culculine's face and Culculine never stopped licking, while the prince collapsed in her wake, prick up arse. Just a few more jerks of the loins, then Mony shot his load. She lay splayed out on the bed while Mony went to wash himself and Culculine got up to piss. She took a chamberpot, stood over it with legs apart, lifted her petticoat and pissed copiously, then, to blow away the last drops clinging to her short-hairs, she let go a soft and discreet little fart which considerably excited Mony.

--- Shit in my hands, shit in my hands! he shouted.

She smiled; he got behind her while she lowered her bum a bit and began to strain. She was wearing a tiny pair of sheer cambric knickers through which could be seen her fine strapping thighs. Black fishnet stockings came up to above her knees and moulded two marvellous calves, exquisitely well-shaped, neither too plump nor too thin. The rump stuck out in this position, admirably framed by the slit in the knickers. Mony looked closely at the two dusky and rosy cheeks, downy, endowed with a plentiful supply of blood. He noted that the base of the spine was rather prominent and below it commenced the crupper-crack. Broad at first, then narrowing and becoming deeper in proportion to the increasing fullness of the buttocks; thus one arrived at the round brown bunghole, tight-furled. The young woman's efforts first made her arsehole dilate and extrude a little skin from within, smooth and pink and akin to a curled lip.

--- Go on, shit! cried Mony.

Soon a small fragment of crap appeared, pointed and insignificant, which showed its head and immediately returned to its cavern. After that it reappeared, followed slowly and majestically by the rest of the sausage which constituted one of the finest turds a large intestine ever produced.

The shit slid unctuous and uninterrupted, ran out unruffled as a ship's cable. It dangled gracefully between the pretty buttocks which were spreading wider and wider. Soon it was swinging more markedly. The arse dilated still more, shook itself a bit and the shit fell, all hot and reeking, into Mony's hands which were held out to receive it. Then he cried: 'Stay like that!' and, leaning over, he licked her arsehole thoroughly while rolling the turd in his hands. Next he squeezed it voluptuously and smeared it all over his body. Culculine was undressing, following the example of Alexine who was stark naked and showing Mony the fat, transparent arse of a blonde. 'Shit on me!' he cried to Alexine, stretching himself out on the floor. She squatted above him, but not wholly, so he could enjoy the spectacle presented by her backside. Her first efforts resulted in forcing out a small quantity of spunk Mony had put there; then came the shit, yellow and soft, which fell in several instalments and, while she was laughing and wriggling, the shit was falling here and there all over the body of Mony, whose belly was soon adorned with several of these odoriferous slugs.

Alexine had pissed at the same time and the steaming jet, playing onto Mony's prick, had reawakened his animal spirits. His shaft began gradually to stir, swelling until the moment when the glans, having reached its normal size, red as a plump plum, stood stiff under the gaze of the young woman who, nearing it, squatted lower and lower, getting the erect prick to penetrate between the hairy verges of her wide open cunt. Mony was revelling in the spectacle. Alexine's arse, as it descended, displayed more and more of its appetizing rotundity. Its enticing curves became fuller and the spread of the buttocks more and more accentuated. When the arse was quite lowered, with the cock completely engulfed, the arse rose up again and began a fetching see-saw motion which modified its volume in its main proportions and this was a delicious spectacle. Mony, covered in shit, was steeped in deepest joy; soon he felt her vagina clench tight and Alexine said in a strangled voice:

--- Bastard, it's coming... I'm coming! and she spilled her spend. But Culculine who had watched this operation and seemed on heat, dragged her roughly off the stake impaling her and, flinging herself on Mony without worrying about the shit that soiled her too, stuffed his staff into her cunt with a sigh of satisfaction. She started bucking her arse ferociously, grunting 'Huh!' for every thrust of the loins. But Alexine, vexed at being cheated of her chattels, opened a drawer and extracted from it a cat-o'-nine-tails made with leather thongs. She began to thrash Culculine on the arse, whose bum-buckings were becoming ever more passionate. Alexine, excited by the spectacle, was smiting heartily and hard. Blows rained on the superb posterior. Mony, leaning his head a little to one side, was watching in a mirror opposite him the rise and fall of Culculine's fat arse. As they rose the buttocks half-opened and the rosebud would momentarily appear, to disappear on the descent when the beautiful chubby cheeks tightened. Below, the hairy and distended lips of her cunt engulfed the enormous prick which, during the ascent, would appear to view almost entire and glistening. Alexine's blows had soon completely reddened the hapless backside which was now quivering with lustful pleasure. Soon one blow left a bleeding weal. Both of them, the whipper and the whipped, became as delirious as Bacchantes and each seemed to be enjoying it quite as much as the other. Mony himself began to share their fury and his nails raked Culculine's satin back. Alexine, to thrash Culculine conveniently, knelt close to the pair. Her big chubby arse, shaking at each blow she dealt, was only inches from Mony's mouth.

35

His tongue was soon inside, then, fraught with lustful fury, he started biting her right buttock. The young girl uttered a cry of pain. The teeth had sunk in and a fresh and vermilion blood came slaking Mony's parched gullet. He lapped it up, much relishing its slightly salty flavour of iron. At this moment, Culculine's bouncing movements became uncontrollable. Her upturned eyes showed only the whites. Her mouth stained with the shit on Mony's body, she let out a moan and discharged at the same time as Mony did. Alexine fell across them exhausted, gasping hoarsely and grinding her teeth, and Mony who put his mouth to her cunt had merely to give two or three licks to obtain a discharge. Then after several convulsions their nerves relaxed, and the trio sprawled in the shit, the blood and the come. They fell asleep like that and when they awoke the bedroom clock was chiming the twelve times for midnight.

--- Don't move, I heard a noise, said Culculine. It's not my maid, she's used to staying out of my way. And she must have gone to bed.

A cold sweat ran down the foreheads of Mony and the two young women. Their hair stood on end and shivers ran through their naked and shit-stained bodies.

--- Someone's there, Alexine declared.

--- Someone is there, Mony agreed.

At this moment the door opened and the little light coming in from the night street allowed them to make out two human shadows clad in overcoats with turned up collars and topped by bowler hats.

The first one abruptly switched on an electric torch he was holding. The beam of light illumined the room, but at first the burglars did not notice the group sprawled over the floor.

--- Phew, smells awful, said the first.

--- Let's go in anyway, must be some gelt in the drawers, replied the second.

Just then Culculine, who had crawled towards the electric light

36

switch, suddenly turned on the light.

The burglars were flabbergasted by all these naked figures:

--- Well shit! said the first, you got good taste, oh yes, Cornaboeux's word on that.

He was a dark hairy-handed colossus. His bushy beard made him even more hideous.

--- What a lark, said the second, for me the shit's all right, it's lucky.

He was a pale one-eyed guttersnipe who was chewing on a dead cigarette butt.

--- You're right, la Chaloupe, said Cornaboeux, I've only just trodden in some and for my first piece of luck I think I'll shag Mademoiselle. But first let's consider the young gent.

And throwing themselves on the startled Mony, the burglars gagged him and bound his arms and legs. Then, turning to the two shivering yet somewhat amused women, la Chaloupe said:

--- And girlies, do try and be nice, or else I'll tell pappa.

He had a cane in his hand and gave it to Culculine, ordering her to beat Mony as hard as she could. Then, placing himself behind her, he pulled out a prick as thin as a little finger, but very long. Culculine was beginning to enjoy herself. La Chaloupe commenced by whacking her buttocks and saying:

--- Well, big bum, you're going to do some shagging; I'm the boy for buggery!

He palped and squeezed this big downy rump and passing one hand round the front of it, fondled the clitoris, then brusquely thrust in the long and thin prick. Culculine started stirring her arse at the same time as thrashing Mony who, unable to defend himself or cry out, wriggled like a worm at each stroke of the stick which left red welts that soon turned purple. Then as the buggery progressed the excited Culculine hit ever harder, shouting:

--- Swine, take that you filthy beast... La Chaloupe, stick your toothpick in deep, all the way.

Soon Mony's body was bleeding.

In the meanwhile Cornaboeux had grabbed hold of Alexine and thrown her onto the bed. He set to by biting her bubs which started to harden. Then he went downward to her cunt and took it all in his mouth while chewing at the pretty, curled blonde bush on her mound. He got up again and took out his short yet enormous prick whose knob was violet. Turning Alexine over, he began spanking her large pink arse; from time to time he would slide his hand into its crack. Then he took the young woman on his left arm so that her cunt was within range of his right hand. The left hand was holding her by her thatch... this was causing her pain. She started crying and her sobs grew louder as Cornaboeux again began slapping her with all his might. Her big pink thighs jiggled about and her arse shuddered each time the burglar's beefy paw landed. In the end she tried to defend herself. Her little hands were free; with them she began clawing at his bearded face. She pulled his beard hairs as he was pulling her merkin's.

--- All right then, said Cornaboeux and he turned her over.

At that moment she caught a glimpse of the spectacle of la Chaloupe buggering Culculine who was beating Mony who was already bleeding all over, and this excited her. Cornaboeux's thick cracksman was now ramming against her rear, but he missed his mark, thwacking to right and left or else a bit too high or too low, then when he did find the hole, he placed his hands on Alexine's sleek and plump loins and tugged her towards him as hard as he could. The pain caused by this enormous prick tearing her arsehole would have made her shriek in agony, had she not been so excited by everything that had just happened. As soon as he had introduced prick to arse, Cornaboeux withdrew it, then, turning Alexine over on the bed again, he sank his instrument into her snatch. The tool entered with great difficulty because of its huge size, but as soon as it was inside, Alexine crossed her legs behind the burglar's haunches and held him so tightly that he could not have withdrawn even had he wanted to. The shagging motion was wild. Cornaboeux was sucking her tits and his beard

38

was tickling and exciting her, so she thrust a hand inside his trousers and stuck one finger in the burglar's swag-hole. Then they began biting each other like wild beasts as they jerked their arses. They discharged frenziedly. But Cornaboeux's cock, nipped by Alexine's vagina, started getting hard again. Alexine closed her eyes, the better to savour this second growing pressure. She discharged fourteen times while Cornaboeux came thrice. When she regained her wits, she noticed that her cunt and her arse were bleeding. They had been wounded by Cornaboeux's enormous root. She caught sight of Mony writhing convulsively on the floor.

His body was an open sore.

Culculine, at the order of the one-eyed la Chaloupe, was sucking his dick, kneeling in front of him.

--- On your feet then, slut! cried Cornaboeux.

Alexine obeyed and he gave her a kick up the arse which sent her sprawling on top of Mony. Cornaboeux bound her arms and legs and gagged her, taking no notice of her entreaties and, seizing the stick, he began to cover with stripes the beautiful body that wasn't as thin as it looked. Her arse quivered under each stroke of the cane, then it was back, belly, thighs, breasts which received the rain of blows. While wriggling and struggling, Alexine met Mony's member, which was rigid as a corpse's. By chance it snagged the young woman's cunt and penetrated.

Cornaboeux redoubled his blows and struck indiscriminately at Mony and Alexine who were in excruciating ecstasy. Soon the young blonde's pretty pink skin was no longer visible below the welts and welling blood. Mony passed out, and she fainted soon afterwards. Cornaboeux, whose arm was beginning to tire, turned towards Culculine, who was still trying to suck off la Chaloupe. But the bugger could not come.

Cornaboeux commanded the beautiful brunette to spread her thighs. He had considerable difficulty fucking her from behind. She suffered greatly but stoically, not letting go of la Chaloupe's prick which she was sucking. When Cornaboeux was in full possession of Culculine's cunt, he made her lift her right arm and bit her underarm hair of which she had a very thick tuft. When the crisis came, it was so intense that Culculine fainted, in violent spasm biting la Chaloupe's prick. He uttered an appalling shriek of agony, but the glans was right off. Cornaboeux, who had just discharged, yanked his bayonet roughly from the cunt of Culculine, who fell fainting to the floor. La Chaloupe was losing blood fast.

--- My poor la Chaloupe, said Cornaboeux, now you're fucked. Be better ending it here and now. And he pulled out a knife and dealt la Chaloupe a mortal blow while shaking over Culculine's body the last drops of spunk that hung from his spigot. La Chaloupe died without so much as a word.

Cornaboeux carefully did up his trousers again, emptied all the money from the drawers and clothing, and took jewellery and watches too. Then he looked at Culculine who lay in a swoon on the floor.

--- I must avenge la Chaloupe, he thought, and, drawing his knife again, struck a terrible blow between Culculine's buttocks, but she remained unconscious. Cornaboeux left the knife in her arse. The clocks struck three a.m. Then he left as he had entered, leaving four bodies stretched out on the floor of a room full of blood, shit, spunk and indescribable disorder.

In the street, he headed briskly for Ménilmontant, singing:

An arse should smell of arse
And not of eau de cologne

and also:

G....arselamp
G....arselamp
Light up, light up, me little bit o' wick.

Chapter Four

The scandal was very considerable. The newspapers discussed this affair for a week. Culculine, Alexine and Prince Vibescu remained bed-ridden for two months. During his convalescence, Mony went one evening to a bar near the Gare Montparnasse. There one drank paraffin, which is a delicious beverage for palates blunted by other liquors.

While sipping the infamous rotgut, the prince stared at the customers. One of them, a bearded colossus, was dressed like a market-porter and his immense flour-covered hat gave him the look of a fabulous demi-god ready to accomplish an heroic labour.

The prince thought he recognized the attractive countenance of the burglar Cornaboeux. Suddenly he heard him order a paraffin in a thunderous voice. It was indeed the voice of Cornaboeux. Mony stood up and went over to him with hand outstretched:

--- How d'you do, Cornaboeux, are you at Les Halles now?

--- Me? said the surprised porter, how do you know me?

--- I saw you at 214 rue de Prony, said Mony with a casual air.

--- It wasn't me, replied Cornaboeux, very dismayed. I don't know you. I've been a porter at Les Halles for three years and they all know me there. Leave me alone!

--- No more nonsense, answered Mony. Cornaboeux, you're mine. I can hand you over to the police. But I like you and if you want to follow along you'll be my valet, you'll go everywhere with me. You can join in on my good times. You'll help me out and protect me if need be. Then, if you're really reliable, I'll make your fortune. Answer at once.

--- You're a good chap and you can't half talk. Shake on it, I'm your man.

Several days later, Cornaboeux, promoted to the rank of valet, was fastening the suitcases. Prince Mony had been recalled post-haste to Bucharest. His intimate friend, the Serbian vice-consul, had just died, leaving him almost all of his worldly goods. It was a question of tin mines, for some years very productive, but which now needed on-the-spot supervision, otherwise the result might be an immediate fall in income. Prince Mony, as we have seen, did not love money for its own sake; he desired to be as rich as possible, but only because of the pleasures that gold alone can procure. He was forever quoting the maxim pronounced by one of his ancestors: 'Everything is for sale; everything can be bought; it's just a matter of setting a price on it.'

Prince Mony and Cornaboeux had taken their seats on the Orient Express; the train's vibration did not fail to make an immediate effect. Mony had a hard-on like a Cossack's and he cast inflamed glances at Cornaboeux. Outside, the admirable countryside of eastern France unfolded its calm and distinct splendours. The saloon car was nearly empty; a gouty old man, richly attired, grizzled away dribbling over *Le Figaro* which he was trying to read.

Mony, who was wrapped in an ample raglan, grasped Cornaboeux's hand and, sliding it through the slit situated in the pocket of this commodious garment, guided it to his fly-buttons. The colossal valet understood his master's wish. His huge hand was hirsute but plump and softer than one would have supposed. Cornaboeux's fingers delicately unbuttoned the prince's trousers. They gripped the raging prick which in all points bore out the famous distich by Alphonse Allais[5]:

The exciting tremor of trains on narrow tracks
Our desires slide as low via the marrow in backs.

But an employee of the Compagnie des Wagons-Lits came in and announced that it was dinner time and many passengers were in the restaurant car.

--- Excellent idea, said Mony. Let's dine first, Cornaboeux!

The hand of the former market-porter emerged from the vent in the raglan. They both headed for the dining car. The prince's prick was still stiff and, since he had not buttoned himself up again, a bulge protuberated to the fore of the garment. Dinner commenced without mishap, rocked by the clanking of the train and the various clinkings of china, silver and crystal, disturbed occasionally by the abrupt pop of a cork from an *Apollinaris.*[6]

At one table opposite, at the far end from where Mony was dining, were two women, blonde and pretty. Cornaboeux, who was facing them, pointed them out to Mony. The prince turned round and recognized the one more modestly dressed; it was Mariette, the exquisite chambermaid from the Grand Hotel. He stood up immediately and made his way towards these ladies. He greeted Mariette and addressed himself to the other young woman who was attractive and heavily rouged. Her hair dyed a peroxide blonde gave her a modern look which entranced Mony:

--- Madame, he said to her, please excuse my approaching you. I am making the introduction myself, owing to the difficulty of finding any mutual acquaintances on this train. I am Prince Mony Vibescu, hereditary hospodar. Mademoiselle here, Mariette I mean, who I dare say has left the service of the Grand Hotel for yours, has kindly put me under an obligation towards her which I wish to repay this very day. I want to marry her to my valet and upon each of them I shall bestow a dowry of fifty thousand francs.

--- I see no objection to that, said the lady, but there's something here which doesn't seem poorly endowed. To whom will you assign it?

Mony's prick had found an outlet and was displaying its rubicund head between two buttons, in front of the prince, who blushed as he stowed the engine from sight. The lady started laughing.

--- Fortunately you were positioned so no-one saw you... that would have made a pretty how-d'ye-do... Do tell me though, who gets this mighty engine?

--- Permit me, said Mony gallantly, to offer it as token of esteem for your sovereign beauty.

--- We'll see about that, said the lady. Meanwhile since you've presented yourself, I'll do so too... Estelle Ronange...

--- The great actress from the *Comédie*[6] asked Mony.

The lady nodded.

Mony, wild with joy, exclaimed:

--- Estelle, I should have recognized you. I've been an ardent admirer of yours for a long time. Haven't I spent evenings at the Théâtre-Français watching you play lovers' parts? And to calm my excitement, not being able to toss off in public, I'd stick my fingers up my nose, pull out the crusty snot and eat it! It was nice! It was good!

--- Mariette, go and have dinner with your fiancé, said Estelle. Prince, dine with me.

As soon as they were sitting facing each other, the prince and the actress gazed at one another amorously.

--- Where are you going? asked Mony.

--- To Vienna, to play before the Emperor.

--- And the Moscow Decree?[7]

--- I don't care a damn about the Moscow Decree; I'm sending in my resignation tomorrow to Claretie... I'm being given the go-by... being made to play bit-parts... they've refused me the role of Eoraka in the new play by our own Mounet-Sully... I'm leaving... They won't stifle my talent.

--- Recite something for me... some poetry, requested Mony.

While the plates were being changed she recited him

L'Invitation Au Voyage. As the admirable poem, wherein Baudelaire has placed a hint of his amorous melancholy and his passionate nostalgia, was proceeding, Mony felt the actress's small feet slide right up alongside his legs: under the raglan they reached Mony's prick which was dangling sadly outside his flies. There the feet stopped and, delicately taking the prick between them, they began a rather curious see-saw motion. Suddenly hard, the young man's prick let itself be frigged by the dainty pumps of Estelle Ronange. Soon he began enjoying it and improvised this sonnet, which he recited to the actress, whose footwork did not cease till the final verse:

EPITHALAMIUM

Your hands shall introduce my stallion's fine prong
Into the bloody brothel bared between your thighs
And I'll aver, despite Avinain, right or wrong,
Your love's no use to me unless you come with sighs!

My mouthing at your breasts as white as creamiest cheese
Makes best obeisance, harmless sucks to you.
From my mentula up your female cleft, clean through,
The sperm will fall like gold in sluices. These,

My sweet tart! these champion cheeks that swive my tarse
Won from all pulpous fruits their tasty mysteries,
Then overcame earth's sexless, lowlier rotundity,

Or the moon, so vain each month of her own arse;
And from your eyes spurts, even when they're veiled from me,
This obscure clarity which tumbles from the stars.[9]

And as the prick had arrived at the limit of excitation, Estelle lowered her feet, saying:

--- Prince, let's not have him spitting in the dining car; whatever would they think of us?... Allow me to thank you for the homage paid Corneille at the climax of your sonnet. Even though I'm about to leave the *Comédie-Française*, everything to do with the company forms the subject of my constant concern.

--- But after appearing before Franz-Josef, said Mony, what do you intend doing?

--- My dream, said Estelle, would be to become a cabaret star.

--- Take care! Mony replied. *The obscure Monsieur Claretie who tumbles the stars* will start endless litigation against you.

--- Don't you worry about that, Mony, make up some more verses for me before we go to bye-bye.

--- Very well, said Mony, and he improvised these delicate mythological sonnets:

HERCULES AND OMPHALE

The bum
Of Omphale
Overcome
Flops down.

-- Do you feel
My awesome
Phallus keen?
-- Some machine!

The hound
Splits my seam!...
Real or dream?...

-- Tight hold please!
It's sodomy
By Hercules.

PYRAMUS AND THISBE

Madame is
Thisbe
Swooning :
'Baby!'

Pyramus
Sagging
Shagging:
'Maybe!'

The beauty
Said: 'Oui!'
Then she

Too came,
The same
As he.[10]

--- That's exquisite! delicious! admirable! Mony, you're an absolutely divine poet, come and fuck me in the sleeping car, I'm really fuckable.

Mony settled the bills. Mariette and Cornaboeux were gazing at each other languorously. In the corridor Mony slipped fifty francs to the rail company steward who let the two couples into the same compartment:

--- You'll arrange it with the customs, said the prince to the man in the peaked cap, we've nothing to declare. But be sure to knock on our door a couple of minutes before the frontier crossing.

In the compartment all four stripped to the buff. Mariette was the first one naked. Mony had never seen her in the nude, but he recognized her big round thighs and the forest of short-hairs that shadowed her chubby cunt. Her tits were erecting fully as were the pricks of Mony and Cornaboeux.

--- Cornaboeux, said Mony, bugger me while I futter this pretty filly.

Estelle was much longer undressing and by the time she was starkers, Mony had shafted Mariette's cunt from the rear; she, beginning to enjoy herself, was flailing her fat posterior and making it slap against Mony's belly. Cornaboeux had thrust his short thick knob into the dilated anus of Mony, who was moaning:

--- Beastly train! We shan't be able to keep our balance.

Mariette was clucking like a hen and lurching about as if squiffed.[11]

Mony had put his arms round her and was squeezing her tits. He admired the beauty of Estelle whose harsh hairdo revealed the hand of a skilled hairdresser. This was a modern woman in every sense of the word: waved hair held in place by tortoiseshell combs whose colour went well with the cleverly bleached hair. Her body was charmingly pretty. Her arse was athletic and stuck out in a provocative fashion. Her artfully painted face gave her the piquant air of a high-class harlot. Her breasts drooped a little but this was very becoming, for they were small, svelte and pear-shaped. They were soft and silken to the touch; they put one in mind of a nannygoat's udders and whenever she turned they joggled about like a cambric handkerchief rolled into a ball and bounced upon the hand.

On her mound she had only a little tuft of silky hairs. She got onto the top bunk and, somersaulting down, threw her long sinewy thighs around the neck of Mariette who, having her mistress's pussy here in front of her mouth, began gamahuching it gluttonously, burying her nose between the buttocks and into the bumhole. Estelle had already stuck her tongue up her maid's cunt and was simultaneously sucking the inside of an inflamed quim and Mony's massive member which was thrusting therein with ardour. Cornaboeux was blissfully revelling in this spectacle. His broadsword, sunk to the hilt in the prince's hairy arse, moved slowly to and fro. He let off two or three good farts which stank up the atmosphere while increasing the pleasure of the prince and the two women. Suddenly Estelle started bucking frantically, her arse began to dance in front of the nose of Mariette, whose gobbles and arse-thrusts also gained strength. Estelle was kicking out right and left, her legs sheathed in black silk and her feet in shoes with Louis XV heels. In doing so she dealt Cornaboeux a dreadful blow on the nose; stunned by it, he began to bleed profusely. 'Whore!' yelled Cornaboeux and by way of revenge viciously pinched Mony's arse. The latter, wild with rage, gave Mariette's shoulder an awful bite that caused her to discharge, bawling. The pain was such that she sank her teeth into the cunt of her mistress who hysterically tightened her thighs around the maid's neck.

--- I'm suffocating! gasped Mariette with some difficulty, but no-one heard her.

The thighs locked still tighter. Mariette's face turned purple, her frothing mouth stayed glued to the actress's cunt.

Mony, bellowing, discharged into an inert cunt. Cornaboeux, eyes starting from his head, let go his load up Mony's arse, declaring in a casual tone:

--- If you don't get pregnant, you're not a man!

The four characters had collapsed in a heap. Stretched out on the bunk, Estelle was grinding her teeth and punching out in all directions and flailing her legs. Cornaboeux pissed out of the window. Mony was trying to withdraw his prick from Mariette's cunt. But he couldn't do so. The maid's body no longer moved.

--- Let me get out, Mony was saying and caressing her, then he pinched her buttocks and bit her, but nothing was any use.

--- Spread her legs will you, she's fainted! Mony said to Cornaboeux.

With great difficulty Mony managed to extract his prick from the cunt which had contracted terribly. They tried to bring Mariette round, but nothing was any use.

--- Shit! she's snuffed it, declared Cornaboeux. And it was true, Mariette had died choked by her mistress's legs, she was dead, irremediably dead.

--- Now we're in a fix! said Mony.

--- It's that there slut caused it all, proclaimed Cornaboeux indicating Estelle, who was beginning to calm down. Taking a hairbrush from the actress's travel-case, he started to beat her violently. The bristles stung with every blow. This castigation seemed to excite her enormously.

Just then there was a knock on the door.

--- That's the agreed signal, said Mony, in a few moments we'll be crossing the frontier. Must have a poke, I swore I would, half in France, half in Germany. Stuff the deader.

Mony, prick rising, hurled himself upon Estelle who with legs spread wide received him in her burning cunt, crying:

--- Put it in, deep, right there!... there!...

The jolts of her arse had something demonic about them, and her mouth was drooling spittle which, mingling with the cosmetic, dribbled vilely over her chin and chest; Mony stuck his tongue into her mouth and rammed the handle of the brush up her arsehole. The result of this new sensation was that she bit Mony's tongue so viciously he had to pinch her to the point of drawing blood to make her let go.

Meanwhile, Cornaboeux had turned over the body of Mariette, whose empurpled face was ghastly. He spread her buttocks and laboriously inserted his huge prick into the sodomitical aperture. Then he gave free rein to his natural ferocity. Tuft by tuft his hands ripped out the dead woman's blonde hair. His teeth tore at a back of Arctic whiteness, and the crimson blood which spurted and quickly coagulated looked as if it were spread over snow.

Somewhat before the climax, he inserted his hand into the still warm vulva and, thrusting his whole arm inside, he began to tug at the bowels of the unfortunate chambermaid. At the moment of climax he had already pulled out two metres of entrails and had wrapped them around his waist like a lifebelt.

He discharged, vomiting up his meal, as much from the vibrations of the train as from the emotions he had experienced. Mony had just discharged and was gazing in stupefaction at his valet who was hiccoughing horribly and puking over the wretched corpse. Amid the bloodstained hair, the bowels and blood were mixed with the vomit.

--- You filthy swine! cried the prince, the rape of this dead girl I'd promised you in marriage shall weigh heavily upon you in the Valley of Jehoshaphat.[12] If I weren't so fond of you I'd kill you like a dog.

Cornaboeux stood up bleeding and choking back the last gasps of his vomiting bout. He pointed at Estelle whose eyes were gazing wide with horror at the repulsive spectacle:

--- She's the cause of it all, he declared.

--- Don't be hard on her, said Mony, she gave you the opportunity to satisfy your necrophiliac inclinations.

And as they were crossing a bridge, the prince went to the window to contemplate the romantic panorama of the Rhine which was unfolding its verdant splendours and unwinding in wide meanders as far as the horizon. It was four o'clock in the morning, cows were grazing in the meadows, children already dancing under German linden trees. The music of fifes, monotonous and dirgeful, heralded the presence of a Prussian regiment, and the strains mingled sadly with the iron clank of the bridge and the muffled accompaniment of the moving train. Contented villages enlivened the riverbanks dominated by age-old donjons and the Rhenish vines displayed ad infinitum their regular and precious mosaic.

When Mony turned round, he saw the sinister Cornaboeux sitting on Estelle's face. His colossal arse covered the actress's face. He had shat and the loathsome and slimy crap was spattered everywhere.

He was holding an enormous knife and with it was labouring

over her palpitating belly. The body of the actress went into brief convulsions.

--- Wait, said Mony, stay sitting there.

And lying on top of the dying woman he slipped his stiffening prick into the moribund cunt. Thus he enjoyed the final spasms of the murdered woman, whose last throes must have been appalling, and he steeped his arms in the hot blood spouting from her belly. When he had discharged, the actress was no longer moving. She was stiff and her staring eyes were filled with shit.

--- Now, said Cornaboeux, we have to scarper.

They cleaned themselves up and dressed. It was six o'clock in the morning. They clambered out of the carriage door and boldly laid themselves flat along the footboard of the train now hurtling full speed ahead. Then, at a signal from Cornaboeux, they let themselves fall smoothly onto the ballast of the railroad bed. They rose to their feet somewhat shaken, but none the worse for wear, and resolutely waved farewell to the train which was already receding into the distance.

--- Nick of time! said Mony.

They reached the next town, stayed two days there, then took train again for Bucharest.

The double murder on the Orient Express supplied the papers with news for six months. The murderers were not found and the crime was attributed to Jack the Ripper, whose back's broad enough.

In Bucharest, Mony came into the property left by the Serbian vice-consul. His connections with the Serbian colony were such that one night he received an invitation to spend an evening at the house of Natacha Kolowitch, the wife of a colonel imprisoned for his hostility towards the Obrenovitch dynasty.[13]

Mony and Cornaboeux arrived at about eight in the evening. The lovely Natacha was in a room draped in black, lit by yellow tapers and decorated with shinbones and skulls.

--- Prince Vibescu, said the lady, you're going to attend a secret session of the anti-dynastic committee of Serbia. We'll no doubt be voting tonight for the death of the infamous Alexander and his whore of a wife, Draga Machine; it's a case of re-establishing the king, Peter Karageorgevitch, on the throne of his ancestors. If you reveal what you see and hear, an invisible hand will kill you wherever you may be.

Mony and Cornaboeux bowed. The conspirators arrived one by one. André Bar, the Parisian journalist, was life and soul of the plot. He arrived, funereal, enveloped in a Spanish cloak.[14]

The conspirators all stripped naked and the lovely Natacha displayed her marvellous nudity. Her arse was gleaming and her belly disappeared beneath a shaggy black fleece that ascended to her navel.

She lay down on a table covered with a black sheet. An Orthodox priest entered clad in sacerdotal vestments. He arranged the sacred vessels and began to say mass on Natacha's belly. Mony happened to be near Natacha; she seized his prick and started sucking it as the mass progressed. Cornaboeux had flung himself on André Bar and was buggering him while the latter held forth lyrically:

--- I swear by this enormous prick which thrills me to the bottom of my ah, soul, that the Obrenovitch dynasty must become extinct ere long. Shove, Cornaboeux! Your buggery's giving me a hard-on.

Placing himself behind Mony, he buggered him while the latter discharged his spunk into the mouth of the lovely Natacha. At this sight, all the conspirators took to buggering each other frenziedly. In that room, naught but wiry male bums impaled on formidable knobs.

The Orthodox priest twice had Natacha toss him off and his ecclesiastical spunk was spattered across the body of the lovely lady wife of the colonel.

--- Bring in the bride and groom! cried the priest.

A strange couple was shown in: a small boy of ten clad in tails, his topper under his arm, accompanied by a ravishing little girl of eight at most; she was wearing a wedding dress, her white satin gown adorned with sprays of orange blossom.

The priest delivered a sermon and married them by an exchange of rings. Then they were urged to engage in fornication. The lad pulled out a wee winkle akin to a little finger and the newly-wed bride hoisting her flounced skirts showed her tiny white thighs at the top of which gaped a small hairless slit pink as the interior of the open beak of a newborn nuthatch. A religious silence descended upon the assembly. The lad strove to screw the lass. As he could not manage it, his trousers were taken off and, to excite him, Mony spanked him nicely while Natacha titillated his little knob and testiclettes with the tip of her tongue. The little boy started a stand and could thus deflower the little girl. When they had been shafting for ten minutes they were separated and Cornaboeux, grasping the lad, stove in his fundament by means of his powerful bayonet. Mony could not contain his desire to poke the little girl. He took hold of her, set her astride his thighs and forced into her minuscule vagina his lively plunger. The two children uttered frightful cries and blood ran down the pricks of Mony and Cornaboeux.

Next the little girl was placed atop Natacha and the priest who had just finished mass raised her skirts and began to thrash her white and charming little arse. Then Natacha stood up again and, straddling André Bar who was seated in an armchair, she skewered herself upon the plotter's enormous prick. They commenced a vigorous St. George, as the English have it.

The little lad, kneeling in front of Cornaboeux, fellated the latter's lance and shed scalding tears as he did so. Mony was buggering the little girl who was struggling like a rabbit about to have its throat cut. The other conspirators were buggering one another with awful grimaces. Then Natacha got up and, turning round, proffered her arse for all the conspirators who came and kissed it one by one. At this moment a wet-nurse with the face of a madonna was led in, her enormous paps swollen with an abundance of milk. She was made to get down on all fours and the priest began to milk her like a cow into the sacred vessels. Mony buggered the wet-nurse, the resplendent whiteness of whose arse was stretched fit to split. The little girl was made to piss so as to fill the chalices. The conspirators then took communion in both kinds, milk and piss.

Then, seizing the shinbones, they swore the death of Alexander Obrenovitch and his wife Draga Machine.

The evening concluded in an infamous fashion. Some old women, the youngest of whom was seventy-four, were brought up and the conspirators fucked them in every manner conceivable. Mony and Cornaboeux retired in disgust around three in the morning. After returning home the prince stripped to the buff and offered his handsome arse to the cruel Cornaboeux who buggered him eight times in succession without pulling out. They used to call these daily sessions their keen little poker-games.

For some time Mony led this monotonous life in Bucharest. The King of Serbia and his wife were assassinated in Belgrade. Their murder belongs to history and has ·already been diversely analysed. The war between Japan and Russia broke out afterwards.

One morning, Prince Mony Vibescu, stark naked and handsome as the Belvedere Apollo, was 69ing with Cornaboeux. Both were gluttonously sucking their respective sugarsticks and lecherously weighing up cylinders that had nothing to do with phonographs. They discharged simultaneously and the prince had his mouth full of spunk when an English flunkey, all very proper, entered bearing a letter on a silver-gilt salver.

The letter announced to Prince Vibescu that he had been ranked lieutenant in Russia, on foreign commission, in the army of General Kouropatkin.

The prince and Cornaboeux manifested their enthusiasm by

mutual buggerings. They then equipped themselves and headed for St. Petersburg before joining their unit.

--- The war suits me fine, declared Cornaboeux, and the arses of the Japanese must be tasty.

--- The cunts of the Japanese women are certainly delectable, added the prince, twiddling his moustache.

Chapter Five

--- His Excellency General Kokodryoff cannot receive visitors at present. He's dipping his sippet into his boiled egg.

--- But I am his aide-de-camp, replied Mony to the concierge. You Petropolitan types are ridiculous with your continual suspections...[15] You see my uniform! My being summoned to St. Petersburg was not, I assume, in order to have to endure the snubs of caretakers?

--- Show me your papers! said the old grouser, a colossal Tartar.

--- There! the prince curtly proclaimed, sticking his revolver under the nose of the terrified door-keeper who grovelled to let the officer pass.

Mony climbed rapidly (purposely clinking his spurs) to the first floor of the palace of General the Prince Kokodryoff, with whom he was to leave for the Far East. Not a soul was about and Mony, who'd seen his general only the previous evening at the Tsar's, was astonished at this reception. Yet the general had fixed the appointment with him and this was the exact time agreed.

Mony opened a door and went into a large dark and deserted drawing-room which he crossed, murmuring:

--- Well, too bad, in for a penny in for a pound. Let's go on and take a look-see.

He opened a new door which closed of its own accord behind him. He found himself in a room even darker than the previous one.

A soft female voice said in French:

--- Fédor, is that you?

--- Yes, it's I, my love! was the *sotto voce* but resolute reply from Mony, whose heart was pounding fit to burst.

He advanced rapidly in the voice's direction and found a bed. A woman was lying on it, fully clothed. She clasped Mony passionately, darting her tongue into his mouth. The latter responded to her caresses. He lifted up her skirts. She spread her thighs. Her legs were bare and a delicious scent of verbena emanated from her satin skin, mingled with the effluvia of the *odor di femina*. Her cunt where Mony laid hand on it was moist. She was murmuring:

--- Let's fuck... I can't stand it any longer... Naughty chap, it's a week since you were here last.

But instead of replying Mony had pulled out his menacing prick and, fully armed, he scaled the bed and rammed his livid bayonet into the hairy breach of the stranger, who immediately wriggled her buttocks, saying:

--- Go right in... You're making me come...

At the same time she put her hand to the base of the member futtering her and began to palp the two small balls that serve as appendages and are called testicles not, as is commonly thought, because they attest to the consummation of the carnal act but rather because they are the diminutive heads harbouring the vertebral matter that spurts from the mentula or lower intelligence, just as the head contains the grey matter of the brain which is the seat of all mental functions.[16]

The stranger's hand was carefully fondling Mony's bollocks. All of a sudden, she let out a scream and with a heave of her arse dislodged her fucker:

--- You're deceiving me, sir, she cried, my lover has three!

She leapt from the bed, pressed an electrical switch and the light came on.

The room was simply furnished: a bed, chairs, a table, a dressing table, a stove. There were several photographs on the table and one represented a brutal-looking officer clad in the uniform of the Preobrajenski regiment.

The stranger was tall. Her beautiful chestnut hair was somewhat dishevelled. Her open bodice disclosed a full bosom comprised of two white blue-veined breasts snugly reposing in a nest of lace. Her petticoats were chastely lowered. Standing there, her countenance simultaneously registering anger and stupefaction, she stayed facing Mony who was seated on the bed, prick in air and hands crossed upon the hilt of his sabre.

--- Monsieur, said the young woman, your insolence is worthy of the country you serve. Never would a Frenchman have had the caddishness to take advantage, as you did, of such an unexpected situation. Get out, I'm ordering you.

--- Madame or Mademoiselle, replied Mony, I am a Romanian prince, a new staff officer of Prince Kokodryoff's. Lately arrived in St. Petersburg, I am ignorant of this city's customs and, despite having an appointment with my superior, I could only gain admission by threatening the porter with my revolver; I believe I'd have been acting churlishly had I not satisfied a woman who appeared to need the feel of a member in her vagina.

--- You might at least have informed me, said the stranger, staring at his virile member which was beating time, that you weren't Fédor. And now be off with you.

--- Alas! cried Mony, and yet you're a Parisienne, you oughtn't to be a prude... Ah! who'll bring me back Alexine Mangetout and Culculine d'Ancône?

--- Culculine d'Ancône! exclaimed the young woman, you know Culculine? I'm her sister, Hélène Verdier; Verdier's also her real name, and I'm governess to the general's daughter. I've a lover, Fédor. He has three balls.

At that moment a great uproar rose from the street. Hélène went to look. Mony watched from behind her. The Preobrajenski regiment was going by. The band was playing an old air to which the soldiers sang dismally:

Oh may your mother be fucked!
Poor yokel, you push off to war,
Your wife'll get herself stuffed
By bulls bursting out of your byre.
As for you boy, they'll tickle your prick,
Siberian flies will, just wait.
On Friday don't give 'em your cock
For it's meatless we go on that day,
Nor sugar, as sugar is off,
It's made from the bones of the dead.
Brothers let's fuck, farmer boys fuck
The cunt of the officer's mare.
She ain't so large in the private parts
As what you find in the Tartar tarts.
Oh may your mother be fucked!

Suddenly the music stopped. Hélène called out. An officer turned his head. Mony, who had just seen his photograph, recognized Fédor, who saluted with his sabre, shouting:

--- Farewell, Hélène, I'm off to the war... We'll never see each other again.

Hélène turned deathly pale and fell fainting into Mony's arms. He carried her to the bed.

He first removed her bodice and her breasts sprang out erect. These were a superb pair of tits with pink nipples. He sucked them a while, then undid her skirt, which he took off together with the petticoats and corset. Hélène stayed in her chemise. Mony very excitedly raised the white material that concealed the incomparable treasures of two faultless legs. The stockings went halfway up her thighs and the thighs were round as ivory towers. At the base of her belly the mysterious grotto was hidden within a sacred wood, fawn like the autumns. This thicket was bushy and the tight lips of the cunt allowed but a glimpse of a groove resembling a mnemonic notch on the poles the Incas used as calendars.

Mony respected Hélène's fainting-fit. He took off her stockings and began to play ten little piggies. Her feet were pretty, chubby as a baby's. The prince's tongue started on the toes of the right foot. Conscientiously he cleaned the big toenail, then slid between the toes. He dwelt a long time on the little toe which was darling, quite darling. He found out that the right foot tasted of raspberry. The licking tongue next truffled into the creases of the left foot, whereon Mony located a flavour reminiscent of Mainz ham.

At this moment Hélène opened her eyes and stirred. Mony stopped his little piggy exercises and watched the tall plump beauty stretch herself in pandiculation. Her mouth opening to yawn showed a pink tongue between neat ivory teeth. Then she smiled.

HELENE. --- Prince, whatever have you been doing to me?

MONY. --- Hélène! it was for your own good that I made you more comfortable. I've been a good Samaritan to you. A good turn is never in vain and I've found an exquisite reward in the contemplation of your charms. You are exquisite and Fédor's a lucky dog.

HELENE. --- I'll never see him again, alas! The Japanese are going to kill him.

MONY. --- I'd really like to replace him but, unfortunately, I do not have three balls.

HELENE. --- Don't talk like that, Mony, it's true you haven't three of them, but what you do have is just as good as his.

MONY. --- Is that true, little piggy? Wait till I unbuckle my swordbelt... That's it. Show me your arse... how big, round and chubby it is... Like a cherub puffing... Well, I'll have to spank you in honour of your sister Culculine... slip, slap, patty whack...

HELENE. --- Oh! oh! ouch! You're hotting me up, I'm sopping

wet.

MONY. --- What a thick thatch you've got... slip, slap... I absolutely must make your big bumface blush. Hey, he's not angry, and when you joggle him a bit he looks quite jolly.

HELENE. --- Come nearer so I can unbutton you, show him to me, this big baby who wants to warm himself up again in his mama's womb. How sweet he is! He has a little red head and no hair. Well to be sure, he does have some hairs down below at the roots and they're hard and black... What a handsome orphan he is... put him in me, ah Mony! I want to suckle him, suck him, make him spurt...

MONY. --- Wait while I give you a little lick of arse...

HELENE. --- Ah! so good, I feel your tongue in the crack of my arse... It's going in and rummaging my rose-folds. Please don't unpleat my poor arsehole too much, eh Mony? There! I'm spreading it well for you. Ah! you've stuck your whole face up my bum... Watch it, I'm farting... Sorry, I couldn't hold it back!... Ah! your moustache is prickly and you're slobbering... pig... you're slobbering. Give it here, give me your big cock to suck... I'm thirsty...

MONY. --- Ah! Hélène how clever your tongue is. If you teach spelling as well as you trim quills you must make a topping teacher... Oh! you're pecking at my knobhole with your tongue... Now I feel it go under the end of the knob... you're cleaning its crease with your hot tongue... Ah! peerless fellatrix, gobbler beyond compare!... Don't suck so hard. You've got my whole knob in your little mouth. You're hurting me... Ah! Ah! Ah! Ah! You're tickling the whole of my prick... Ah! Ah! Don't squeeze my balls... your teeth are sharp... That's it, get the tip of the head again, that's where to work...You like knob a lot, don't you?... little sow... Ah! Ah!... Ah!... Ah!... I'm...co...coming... pig... she's gulped the lot... Here, give me your big cunt so I can suck you off while I'm getting another hard-on...

HELENE. --- Press harder... Move your tongue about right on my button... Do you feel my clitoris swelling... listen, give me the bowling grip... that's it... Push your thumb well into my cunt and your index finger up my arse. Ah! that's good... that's good!... There, do you hear my tummy rumble with pleasure... That's it, your left hand on my left titty... crush the strawberry... I'm coming... Ooh! can you feel my arse working, my fucking movements... bastard! that's good... come and fuck me. Give me your prick to suck, quick, so I can make it stiff and hard again, let's do 69, you on top...

You've got a stand you swine, that didn't take long, screw me... Wait, some hairs have got stuck. Suck my tits... like that, that's good!... Get right in deep... there, stay like that, don't move... I've got you tight... I'm tightening my bottom... I'm about to... I'm dying... Mony... my sister, did you make her come so much?... push hard... that's going so deep, right into my soul... it's making me come like dying...I can't stand it any longer... dear Mony... let's let go together. Ah! I can't wait any more, it's all pouring out of me... I'm coming...

Mony and Hélène discharged at the same time. Then he cleaned her cunt with his tongue and she did the same for his prick.

While he tidied himself up and Hélène dressed again they heard a woman's cries of pain.

--- It's nothing, said Hélène, Nadia's being beaten: she's Wanda's chambermaid. Wanda's the general's daughter, my pupil.

--- This scene I'd like to watch, said Mony.

Hélène, half-dressed, led Mony through a dark unfurnished room whose false interior window was glassed and looked on to a young girl's room. Wanda, the general's daughter, was a quite pretty creature of seventeen. She was brandishing a nagaika with all her might and was flogging a most attractive young blonde who squatted on all fours before her with skirts raised. This was Nadia. Her arse was marvellous, enormous, plump. It swung about below an improbably slim waist. Each stroke of the nagaika made her jump and her arse seemed to distend. It was marked out like a St. Andrew's cross, scars the terrible nagaika was leaving there.

--- Mistress, I won't do it any more, cried the girl being thrashed, and her arse as she rose again to her feet afforded a view of a cunt wide apart and shadowed by a forest of tow-coloured short-hairs.

--- Get out, now, cried Wanda, delivering a kick to Nadia's crutch; the girl ran off howling.

Then the young woman went and opened a small cupboard from which emerged a little girl of thirteen or fourteen, thin, dark and depraved-looking.

--- That's Ida, daughter to the dragoman at the Austro-Hungarian embassy, murmured Hélène in Mony's ear; she frigs with Wanda.

Indeed, the small girl threw Wanda on the bed, lifted her skirts and brought to light a forest of short-hairs, virgin forest still, from which burgeoned a clitoris long as a little finger, which Ida began sucking frantically.

--- Suck hard, Ida dear, said Wanda amorously, I'm very excited and so must you be too. Nothing's as exciting as beating a big bum like Nadia's. No more sucking now... I'm going to fuck you.

The small girl took up position, skirts raised, near the tall one. The latter's legs contrasted singularly with the thin, dark and wiry thighs of the former.

--- It's curious, said Wanda, how I've deflowered you with my clitoris and yet I'm still a virgin.

But the act had commenced, Wanda was clasping her little sweetheart wildly. For a moment she caressed the tiny still almost hairless cunt. Ida was saying:

--- My little Wanda, my little husband, how hairy you are! fuck me!

Soon a clitoris entered Ida's cleft and the fine plump arse of Wanda bucked furiously.

Mony at this spectacle was quite beside himself and slipped one hand beneath Hélène's skirts and frigged her skilfully. She did him the same service by eagerly grasping his enormous shaft and, while the two tribades embraced frenziedly, she manipulated the officer's fat baton. Foreskin pulled back, the member steamed. Mony braced his knees and energetically nipped Hélène's little button. Suddenly Wanda, red-faced and dishevelled, sprang off her little lover who, seizing a candle still in its stick, completed the work begun by the well-developed clitoris of the general's daughter. Wanda went to the door and called Nadia, who returned, frightened. At her mistress's command, the pretty blonde undid her bodice and brought out her big tits, then lifted her skirts and proffered her arse. Wanda's erected clitoris soon penetrated the satin buttocks between which she worked to and fro like a man. The girl Ida, whose chest now bared was charming but flat, continued with her candle game, seated between the legs of Nadia, whose cunt she skilfully sucked. Mony at that moment discharged under the pressure from Hélène's fingers and the spunk bespattered the glass pane that separated them from the sapphists. They were apprehensive lest their presence be detected, and so made off.

Clasping each other still, they slipped into a corridor.

— What did the porter mean, asked Mony, when he told me the general was 'dipping his sippet into his boiled egg'?

— Look, replied Hélène, and through a half-open door that gave a view into the general's study, Mony espied his commanding officer standing there in the process of buggering a delightful young lad. The latter's curly chestnut locks fell to his shoulders. His blue and angelic eyes held the innocence of the ephebes whom the gods, since they love them, cause to die young. His fine firm white arse seemed to accept, but only with modesty, the virile gift being made him by the general, who somewhat resembled Socrates.

— The general, said Hélène, himself tutors his twelve year old son. The porter's metaphor was not very plain for, rather than feed himself, the general has found this convenient method wherewith to feed and embellish the mind of his male progeny. He instils into him fundamentally a knowledge that seems solid enough to me, and the young prince will later be able without shame to cut a fine dash in the councils of the Empire.

--- Incest, said Mony, produces miracles.

The general seemed at the acme of pleasure, he was rolling bloodshot eyes.

--- Sergei, he cried in a broken voice, do you really feel the instrument which, not satisfied with having begotten you, has also taken on the task of making a perfect young man of you? Remember, Sodom is a civilizing symbol. Homosexuality would have placed men again on a par with the gods, and all misfortunes spring from this desire which opposite sexes pretend to have for one another. There is only one way today of saving our unfortunate and holy Russia, and that is through pederasty, men finally professing Socratic love for the encruppered, while women will go to the rock of Leucadia to take lessons in Sapphism.[17]

And with a wheezing cry of lust, he discharged into the charming arsehole of his son.

Chapter Six

The siege of Port Arthur had begun. Mony and his batman Cornaboeux were surrounded there along with the troops of the courageous Stoessel.

While the Japanese attempted to storm the enceinte reinforced by barbed-wire, the defenders of the position, under constant threat of death by gunfire, would cheer themselves by assiduously frequenting the nightclubs and brothels that had remained open.

This particular evening, Mony had dined heartily in company with Cornaboeux and a few journalists. They had consumed excellent horse-steak, fish caught in the port itself, and canned pineapples; the whole meal washed down with excellent champagne.

As a matter of fact, the dessert had been interrupted by the untimely arrival of a shell which exploded, destroying part of the restaurant and killing several of the guests. Mony was most chipper after this adventure; he had with some coolness lit his cigar from the tablecloth which had caught fire. He and Cornaboeux were headed for a nightclub.

--- That damned General Kokodryoff, he said on the way, remarkable strategist, no doubt about that; he'd predicted the siege of Port Arthur and very likely had me posted here as revenge for surprising him during his incestuous relations with his son. Just like Ovid, I am expiating the crime of my eyes, but I shall write neither *Tristia* nor *Epistles From Pontus*.[18] I prefer to enjoy whatever time is left me.

Several cannon-balls whistled past above their heads; they strode over a sprawling woman cut in half by a projectile and thus arrived outside *Les Délices du Petit Père*.[19]

This was the modish dive of Port Arthur. They went in. The room was filled with smoke. A red-headed German chanteuse, of bulging girth, was singing in a heavy Berlin accent, applauded frantically by those of the spectators who understood German. Next, four English 'girls', the something-or-other 'Sisters', who danced steps of a jig, with variations of cakewalk and maxixe. They were extremely pretty, these girls. They would lift aloft their swishing skirts to display knickers trimmed with frills and furbelows, but luckily the knickers were split and one could sometimes see their big buttocks framed by the cambric, or the short-hairs which shaded the whiteness of their bellies. When they kicked up their legs, their cunts showed all mossy. They were singing:

My cosey corner girl[20]

and were far more applauded than the ridiculous fräulein who had preceded them.

Some Russian officers, probably too poor to buy themselves women, were wanking conscientiously while they gazed wide-eyed at this, in the Mohammedan sense, paradisiac spectacle.

From time to time, a powerful jet of spunk would spurt from one of these pricks to land upon a nearby uniform or even splash a beard.

After *les girls*, the orchestra struck up a resounding march and the star turn took the stage. It consisted of two Spaniards, male and female. Their toreador costumes made a lively impact on the spectators, who broke into an appropriate *Bojé tsaria Krany*.[21]

The Spanish woman was a superb, fetchingly contortionist

creature. Jet-black eyes glistened in her pale, perfectly oval face. Her hips were shapely and the spangles on her costume were dazzling.

The torero, svelte and strong, twisted about a rump whose masculinity was undoubtedly shown off to some advantage.

This interesting pair, left hands resting on thrust out hips, began by blowing to the audience a couple of right-handed kisses that caused a furore. Then they danced lasciviously in the style of their own country. Next the Spanish woman pulled her skirts up to her navel and fastened them so that she remained exposed right up to the umbilical dimple. Her long legs were sheathed in red silk stockings that reached threequarter length up her thighs. There, they were attached to her corset by gilded suspenders to which were tied the silk cords supporting a black velvet patch at her buttocks, thus masking her arsehole. Her cunt was hidden by a clump of curly blue-black hair.

The torero, still singing, took out his very long and very stiff prick. They danced thus, bellies thrust forward, seeming to pursue and retreat. The young woman's belly undulated like a sea suddenly turning firm; thus the Mediterranean foam condensed to form the pure belly of Aphrodite.

Suddenly, and as if by magic, the prick and cunt of these thespians met and it looked as if they might simply be going to copulate onstage.

Not so.

Via his well-endowed prick the torero lifted up the young woman, who bent her legs and no longer touched the ground. He strolled around for a moment. Then the stagehands stretched a wire three metres above the heads of the spectators, he climbed onto it and, obscene tightrope-walker that he was, thus promenaded his mistress over the congested onlookers, right across the hall. Then he was on stage again, walking backwards. The spectators applauded for all they were worth and greatly appreciated the charms of the Spanish woman, whose masked arse

69

seemed to smile, for it was wreathed in dimples.

Then it was the woman's turn. The torero bent his knees and, firmly embedded in his companion's cunt, was also walked along the tightrope.

This funambulatory fancy had excited Mony.

--- Let's go to the brothel, he said to Cornaboeux.

The Merry Samurai, that was the agreeable name of the fashionable bordello during the siege of Port Arthur.

It was run by two men, a pair of old symbolist poets who, after marrying for love in Paris, had come to hide their happiness in the Far East. They plied the lucrative trade of keeping a brothel and did very well out of it. They dressed like women and called themselves tribades without renouncing their moustaches and masculine names.

One was Adolphe Terré. He was the elder. The younger had had his hour of celebrity in Paris. Who does not recall the pearl-grey cloak and ermine collar of Tristan de Vinaigre?[22]

--- We want women, Mony said in French to the girl cashier who was none other than Adolphe Terré. The latter started on one of his poems:

One evening betwixt Versailles and Fontainebleau
I followed a nymph through the rustling forests
My prick straight stiffened bald to seize its chance
Then passing slim and upright diabolically idyllic.
I poked her thrice, was drunk then for three weeks,
Caught a clap but the gods were wont to protect
The poet. Wistarias replaced my short-hairs
And Virgil shat on me, this Versaillian distich...[23]

--- Enough of that, said Cornaboeux, women, for God's sake!
--- Here's the assistant madame! said Adolphe respectfully.

The assistant madame, that's to say the blond Tristan de Vinaigre, swept forward graciously and, flashing his blue eyes at

Mony, declaimed in a singsong voice this historical poem:

> *My prick flushed with vermilion joy*
> *In the heyday of my youth*
> *And my balls swung like weighty fruit*
> *That seek their trug.*
> *The luxuriant fleece wherein my cock is snug*
> *Beds very thickly down*
> *From arse to groin and groin to navel (in fact, on every level!)*
> *While sparing my frail cheeks,*
> *Which are immobile and tense when I need to shit*
> *On table too high and on paper shiny*
> *The hot turds of my thoughts.*

--- Come now, said Mony, is this a brothel or a public convenience?

--- All ladies to the drawing-room! cried Tristan, at the same time handing Cornaboeux a towel and adding:

--- One towel between two, Messieurs... You understand... in time of siege.

Adolphe collected the 360 roubles that it cost for intercourse with prostitutes at Port Arthur. The two friends went into the drawing-room. An incomparable spectacle awaited them there.

The whores, clad in négligées gooseberry-coloured, crimson, mauve or maroon, were playing bridge and smoking Virginia cigarettes.

At that moment, there was a frightful crash: a shell holed the ceiling and fell heavily onto the floor, where it buried itself like a meteor right in the centre of the circle formed by the bridge-players. Fortunately the shell did not explode. The women all fell backwards shrieking. Their legs flailed aloft and they presented the ace of spades to the concupiscent eyes of the two soldiers. It was an admirable array of arses of all nationalities, for this model brothel had whores of every race. The pear-shaped arse of the

Friesian contrasted with the rounded arses of the Parisiennes, the marvellous buttocks of the English, the squarish posteriors of the Scandinavians and the lowslung rumps of the Catalans. One negress displayed a contorted mass which looked more like a volcanic crater than a woman's cruppers. As soon as she was back on her feet she declared that the enemy camp had made a grand slam; thus rapidly do we become used to the horrors of war.

--- I'll take the negress, announced Cornaboeux, while that Queen of Sheba, rising on hearing herself called for, saluted her Solomon with these agreeable words:

--- You gonna stuff mah sweet 'tater, Gen'r'l, sah?

Cornaboeux hugged her pleasantly. But Mony was not satisfied with this international exhibition:

--- Where are the Japanese girls? he demanded.

--- That's fifty roubles extra, declared the assistant madame, twisting up his heavy mustachios. That's the enemy, you realize!

Mony paid up and a score of little molls in their national costume were brought in.

The prince chose a charming one and the assistant madame led the two couples into a retreat-room fitted up for fucking purposes.

The negress was called Cornelia and the moll answered to the delicate name of Kilyemu, meaning flower bud of the loquat; as they undressed one was singing in pidgin-Tripolitan, the other in Bitchlamar.[24]

Mony and Cornaboeux undressed.

The prince left his valet and the negress in one corner and concerned himself only with Kilyemu whose beauty, at once childish and grave, bewitched him.

He embraced her tenderly and, from time to time during this beautiful night of love, one heard the noise of the bombardment. Shells were bursting softly. It was as if an Oriental prince were offering a firework display in honour of some virginal Georgian princess.

Kilyemu was small but very well-made, her body was yellow as a peach, her small and pointed breasts were hard as tennis balls. The short-hairs at her cunt were gathered into a tiny tuft, coarse and black, like the tip of a wetted paintbrush.

She lay on her back and, drawing her thighs up to her belly with knees bent, opened her legs like a book.

This posture, impracticable for a European, astonished Mony.

He soon tasted its charms. His prick sank right up to the balls in a cunt which, wide at first, promptly tightened in an astounding way.

And this little girl who seemed barely nubile had a nutcracker. Mony well appreciated it, when, after the ultimate convulsions of lust, he discharged into a crazily contracted vagina that drained his prick to the last drop...

--- Let's have your story, said Mony to Kilyemu as they were hearing from the corner the brazen gasps of Cornaboeux and the negress.

Kilyemu sat up.

--- I am, she said, the daughter of a *samisen* player. It's a kind of guitar, they play it in the theatre. My father used to represent the chorus and, playing sad tunes, he'd recite lyrical and rhyming stories from a railed stage-box.

My mother, the beautiful July Peach, played the leading roles in those long plays dear to Nipponese dramatic art.

I remember when *The Forty-Seven Rōnin*, *The Beautiful Siguenai*, and also *Taiko* were performed.[25]

Our troupe went from town to town, and the splendid natural scenery amid which I grew up still comes back to me in moments of amorous abandon.

I would climb among the *matsous*, the giant conifers; I'd go and watch the handsome naked Samurai bathing in the rivers; their enormous members held no significance for me in those days, and I would laugh with the pretty and cheerful girl servants who came to dry them.

Oh! to make love in my ever-blossoming land! To love some

well-built wrestler under the pink cherry trees and to walk down the hillsides, arms around each other!

A sailor on leave from the Nippon Josen Kaisha Company, a cousin of mine, took my virginity one day.

My father and mother were playing *The Great Thief* and the house was packed. My cousin took me out for a walk. I was thirteen. He had travelled in Europe and told me the wonders of a world of which I knew nothing. He led me into a deserted garden full of irises, dark red camellias, yellow lilies, and lotuses like my tongue, so pink and pretty. There he kissed me and asked me if I had ever made love and I told him no. Then he undid my kimono and tickled my breasts, which made me laugh, but I became very serious when he put a hard, thick and long thing in my hand.

--- What do you want to do with that? I asked him.

Without replying, he laid me down, uncovered my legs and, darting his tongue into that mouth, he pierced my maidenhead. I had the strength to let out a cry that must have stirred the graminaceae and the lovely chrysanthemums of the deserted garden but, immediately after, sensual pleasure awoke in me.

A gunsmith abducted me then, he was as handsome as the Daibutsu of Kamakura[26], and one must mention with religious awe his rod, which seemed like gilded bronze and was inexhaustible. Every evening before making love I believed myself to be insatiable, but when I'd felt the warm seed pour into my vulva fifteen times, I had to offer him my weary rump so he could satisfy himself like that, or, when I was too fatigued, I'd take his tool in my mouth and suck it till he ordered me to stop! He killed himself in accordance with the code of Bushido, and by accomplishing this knightly act left me alone and inconsolable.

An Englishman from Yokohama picked me up. He smelt like a corpse, like all Europeans, and for a long time I couldn't get used to that odour. Also I would beg him to bugger me so that I wouldn't see before me his bestial face with its ginger sidewhiskers. However in the end I grew accustomed to him and, as he was under my control, I would make him lick my vulva until his tongue got cramp and could no longer move.

A girlfriend whose acquaintance I'd made in Tokyo and whom I loved madly came to console me.

She was pretty as spring and it always seemed as if two bees were resting upon her nipples. We would satisfy each other with a piece of yellow marble carved at both ends in the form of a prick. We were insatiable and, when in one another's arms, wild, frothing and shrieking; we'd flail about furiously like two dogs that want to gnaw the same bone.

The Englishman went mad one day; he thought he was the Shogun and wanted to bugger the Mikado.

They took him away and I worked as a prostitute together with my friend till the day I fell in love with a tall, strong, clean-shaven German who had a big inexhaustible prick. He used to beat me and I would embrace him weeping. Finally, when I was black and blue, he would favour me with his prick and I'd come like one possessed, gripping it with all my strength.

One day we boarded a boat, he took me off to Shanghai and sold me to a procuress. Then he went away, my handsome Egon, with not even a glance back, leaving me in despair among the brothel women who were laughing at me. They taught me the trade well, but when I have much money I'll go as honest woman, throughout the world, to find my Egon and again feel his shaft in my vulva and die thinking of the trees pink in Japan.

The tiny Japanese woman, neat and serious, went away like a shadow, leaving Mony with tears in his eyes to reflect on the frailty of human passions.

Then he heard a sonorous snoring and, looking round, saw the negress and Cornaboeux chastely asleep in one another's arms, but they were monstrous, both of them. Cornelia's great arse was sticking out, reflecting the moon whose light streamed in through the open window. Mony unsheathed his sabre and prodded this great hunk of meat.

Shouts came from the drawing-room, also. Cornaboeux and Mony sallied forth with the negress. The drawing-room was full of smoke. Several coarse and drunken Russian officers had entered, spewing vile obscenities, and had thrown themselves on the English whores who, repelled by the disgraceful appearance of these old troopers, vied with each other in muttering *Bloodys* and *Damns*.

Cornaboeux and Mony for a moment contemplated the rape of the whores, then during a collective and stupendous buggeration departed, leaving the desperate Adolphe and Tristan de Vinaigre striving to restore order and fruitlessly fluttering about, hampered by their petticoats.

At that very moment General Stoessel entered and everyone, the negress included, had to correct dress and demeanour.

The Japanese had just delivered the first assault on the besieged town.

Mony was almost of a mind to retrace his steps and see what his commander would do, but savage yells were heard from the ramparts.

Soldiers arrived leading a prisoner. He was a tall young man, a German they'd found at the outer perimeter of the defences, busy looting corpses. He was shouting in German:

--- I'm not a thief. I love the Russians, I came bravely through the Japanese lines to offer myself as an arse-pedlar, a sod, a bumboy. You must be short of women and you won't complain having me.

--- Death! cried the soldiers, put him to death, he's a spy, a looter, thieving off the dead!

No officer was accompanying the soldiers. Mony stepped forward and demanded explanations:

--- You're mistaken, he said to the foreigner, we have women aplenty but your crime must be avenged. You're going to be buggered, since you're so keen on it, by the soldiers who captured you, and after that you'll be impaled. Thus you'll die as you have lived, which is, according to the moralists, the finest death. Your name?

--- Egon Müller, declared the man, trembling.

--- All right, said Mony drily, you come from Yokohama, and like a true pimp you shamefully peddled your mistress, a Japanese girl called Kilyemu. Sod, spy, pimp and corpse-robber, you're the whole boiling. Prepare the stake, soldiers and you bugger him... You don't get a chance like this every day.

The handsome Egon was stripped naked. He was an admirably handsome lad and his breasts were rounded like those of a hermaphrodite. At the sight of these charms, the soldiers pulled out their concupiscent pricks.

Cornaboeux was touched; with tears in his eyes he begged his master to spare Egon, but Mony was inflexible and would only allow his orderly to have his cock sucked by the charming ephebe with arse braced, the latter receiving in turn into his dilated anus the glistening knobs of the soldiers who, like the simple brutes they were, sang religious anthems by way of celebrating their capture.

The spy, after receiving the third discharge, began coming furiously and as he was sucking Cornaboeux's prick, bucked his bum about as if he still had thirty years of life ahead of him.

Meanwhile they had erected the iron stake which was to serve as seat for the sodomist.

When all the soldiers had buggered the prisoner, Mony had a few words in the ear of Cornaboeux, who was still blissful from the sucking off just vouchsafed him.

Cornaboeux went over to the brothel and soon returned thence accompanied by the young Japanese harlot Kilyemu, who was wondering what they wanted of her.

She suddenly caught sight of Egon who had just been slung, gagged, onto the iron stake. He was writhing around and the spike was penetrating inch by inch into his fundament. His penis stood out stiff as if fit to burst.

Mony pointed out Kilyemu to the soldiers and the poor little woman stared at her spitted lover with eyes in which terror, love and pity mingled in a supreme desolation. The soldiers stripped her naked and hoisted her wretched little birdlike body onto that of the impaled man.

They spread apart the unfortunate woman's legs and the distended prick she had so desired penetrated her once more.

The poor simple little soul did not understand this barbarity, but the prick which was filling her excited her to the point of crisis. She turned into a mad thing and flailed around, making her lover's body slide gradually down the length of the stake. He discharged while dying.

Here was a strange standard indeed, comprised of this gagged man and the woman writhing astride him, lips split!... Dark blood was forming a puddle at the foot of the stake.

--- Soldiers, salute the dying, cried Mony, and then, addressing Kilyemu:

--- I have fulfilled your desires... At this very moment the cherry trees are in blossom in Japan, lovers are wandering in the pink snow of scattered petals!

Then, levelling his revolver, he shot her in the head and the brains of the little courtesan spurted into the officer's face as if she had wished to spit on her executioner.

Chapter Seven

After the summary execution of the spy Egon Müller and the Japanese whore Kilyemu, Prince Vibescu became very popular in Port Arthur.

One day, General Stoessel sent for him and handed him an envelope, saying:

--- Prince Vibescu, although you are not Russian, you are nonetheless one of the best officers in the fort... We are awaiting relief, but General Kouropatkin must make haste... If he's any longer we shall have to capitulate... These Japanese dogs are lying in wait for us and their fanaticism will some day soon overcome our resistance. You must cross the Japanese lines and deliver this dispatch to the generalissimo.

A balloon was prepared. For a week Mony and Cornaboeux practised handling the aerostat, which was inflated one fine morning.

The two messengers climbed into the basket, pronounced the traditional: 'Cast off!' and soon, after reaching the region of the clouds, the earth appeared to them as only a small thing, the theatre of war clearly visible with the armies and the fleets at sea, while a match which they struck to light their cigarettes left a trail more luminous than the giant cannon-balls employed by the belligerents.

A fresh breeze pushed the balloon in the direction of the

Russian armies and after a few days they landed and were received by a tall officer who bade them welcome. It was Fédor, the man with three balls and the former lover of Hélène Verdier, sister to Culculine d'Ancône.

--- Lieutenant, said Prince Vibescu to him as he jumped out of the basket, you're a gentleman and the reception you've given us makes up for many hardships. Allow me to beg your pardon for cuckolding you in St. Petersburg with your mistress Hélène, the French governess to General Kokodryoff's daughter.

--- You did the right thing, retorted Fédor, and just imagine, I've found her sister Culculine here; she's a superb girl, works as kellnerine in a brasserie with women which our officers frequent.[27] She left Paris to seek her fortune in the Far East. She's making a great deal of money here, since the officers act like men without very long to live and go out on the spree. And her friend Alexine Mangetout is with her.

--- What! cried Mony, Culculine and Alexine are here!... Take me quickly to General Kouropatkin, first I must accomplish my mission... Then take me to the brasserie.

General Kouropatkin received Mony amiably in his palace. This was a rather well-furnished railway carriage.

The generalissimo read the message, then said:

--- We shall do everything in our power to relieve Port Arthur. Meanwhile, Prince Vibescu, I appoint you a Knight of St. George...

Half an hour later, the newly decorated one found himself in *The Sleeping Cossack* brasserie in the company of Fédor and Cornaboeux. Two women hastened to serve them. It was the utterly delightful Culculine and Alexine. They were dressed up as Russian soldiers and wore lace aprons over their baggy breeches which were tucked into their boots; their arses and their breasts protruded pleasantly thus and filled out the uniform. A little cap perched sideways on the hair completed this excitingly military attire. They looked like walk-on parts in some operetta.

--- Well, if it isn't Mony! cried Culculine.

The prince kissed the two women and asked them for their story.

--- Right you are, said Culculine, but you must tell us what's happened to you, too.

Since that fatal night when the burglars left us half dead by the body of the one whose prick I bit off in a fit of wild abandon, I came round only to find myself surrounded by doctors. I'd been found with a knife stuck in my bum. Alexine was taken care of at her place and we heard no further news of yourself. But when we were up and about again, we learned you had gone back to Serbia. The affair caused a tremendous scandal, my explorer dropped me when he returned and Alexine's senator wouldn't keep her any longer.

Our star was beginning to wane in Paris. The war broke out between Russia and Japan. The pimp of one of my girlfriends was organizing a contingent of women to serve in the brasserie-brothels which would follow the Russian army, we were hired and that's it.

Mony then recounted what had happened to him, omitting what had taken place on the Orient Express. He introduced Cornaboeux to the two women but without saying he was the burglar who had stuck his knife into Culculine's buttocks.

All these narrations induced an ample consumption of beverages. The room was full of officers in caps who were singing at the tops of their voices and fumbling the waitresses.

--- Let's go, said Mony.

Culculine and Alexine followed them and the five military types left the entrenchments and headed for Fédor's tent.

The night had become starry. When passing the generalissimo's coach, Mony on a whim made Alexine, whose big buttocks seemed constrained in the breeches, tug them off and, while the others continued their walk, he handled the superb arse that resembled a pale face under the pale moon, then, pulling out his grim instrument he frotted it a moment in the arse's cleft,

81

occasionally pecking at the arsehole; then, hearing an incisive bugle call accompanied by drum rolls, he suddenly decided. His tool descended between the cool buttocks and entered a valley that ended at the cunt. In front, the young man's hands fingered fleece and fluttered clitoris. He moved to and fro, trenching with his ploughshare the furrow of an Alexine who got pleasure from wriggling her lunar arse upon which the moon above seemed to smile in admiration. Suddenly the monotonous call of the sentries began; their cries were to be repeated throughout the night. Alexine and Mony came silently and when they ejaculated, almost simultaneously and sighing deeply, a shell tore through the air and killed several soldiers sleeping in a ditch. They died wailing like children calling for their mother. Mony and Alexine, quickly tidying themselves up, ran to Fédor's tent.

There they found Cornaboeux, his flies undone, kneeling in front of Culculine who, sans breeches, was showing him her arse. He was saying:

--- No, it doesn't show at all and nobody'd ever know you'd been stabbed on it.

Then, rising to his feet he buggered her shouting out some Russian phrases he had learned.

Fédor positioned himself in front of her and inserted his organ into her cunt. One might have thought Culculine was some pretty boy being buggered while he dipped his wick in a woman. She was indeed dressed like a man and Fédor's tool seemed part of her. But her buttocks were too broad for such a notion to prevail for long. Likewise her slim waist and the curve of her breast belied her being a bumboy. The trio was bobbing about in rhythm and Alexine approached it to tickle Fédor's three balls.

At that moment from outside the tent a soldier called loudly for Prince Vibescu.

Mony went out; the serviceman had come as courier for General Munin who was summoning Mony forthwith.

He followed the soldier and, crossing the encampment, they

arrived at a rail wagon into which Mony climbed as the soldier announced:

--- Prince Vibescu.

The interior of the wagon resembled a boudoir, but an Oriental boudoir. Extravagant luxury was the order of the day there, and General Munin, a gigantic fifty year old, received Mony with considerable courtesy.

He pointed out to him a pretty woman of about twenty, nonchalantly lying on a sofa.

She was a Circassian, his wife.

--- Prince Vibescu, said the general, my wife, hearing talk of your exploit today, was bent on congratulating you. Then again, she's three months pregnant and a pregnant woman's craving is irresistibly driving her to a desire to sleep with you. Here she is! Do your duty. I shall satisfy myself in another manner.

Without replying, Mony stripped and started to undress the fair Haïdyn who seemed in a state of extraordinary excitement. She bit at Mony while he was undressing her. She was admirably proportioned and her pregnancy did not yet show. Her breasts, moulded by the Graces, thrust up round as cannon-balls.

Her body was supple, sleek and slender. There was such a nice disproportion between the plumpness of her arse and the slenderness of her waist that Mony felt his member stand up like a Norway spruce.

She seized hold of it while he palped her thighs, which were plump at the top and tapering down towards the knee.

When she was nude, he mounted her and, neighing like a stallion, shafted her while she closed her eyes, savouring an infinite bliss.

General Munin, meanwhile, had had a small Chinese lad brought in, very sweet and scared.

His slit eyes blinked catching sight of the couple in the act.

The general undressed him and sucked his pricklet that was scarcely as big as a jujube.

Then he turned him round and spanked his skinny little yellow bottom. He grasped his great sabre and set it beside him.

He then buggered the little boy who must have been familiar with this manner of civilizing Manchuria, for he was wriggling his celestial bumboy's body in skilful style.

The general was saying:

--- Have a good come, Haïdyn my dear, I'm going to come too.

And his prick pulled almost completely out of the Chinese child's body to re-enter promptly. When he had reached the climax, he took the sabre and, clenching his teeth and without ceasing the buggery, cut the head off the little Chinese, whose last spasms procured him a huge ejaculation while blood spouted from his neck like water from a fountain.

The general then withdrew from the arsehole and wiped his tool with his handkerchief. He next cleaned his sabre and, picking up the boy's decollated head, presented it to Mony and Haïdyn who had now changed position. The Circassian was riding Mony with furious abandon. Her tits danced and her arse bucked frenziedly. Mony's hands kneaded those marvellous plump buttocks.

--- Look, said the general, how nicely the little Chinese boy smiles!

The head was grimacing horribly, but its look redoubled the erotic frenzy of the two fuckers who bucked arses with yet more ardour.

The general dropped the head, then seizing his wife by the hips inserted his member into her arse. Mony's lustful joy was thereby increased. The two pricks, separated only by a thin membrane, just about butted heads, increasing the pleasure of the young woman, who was biting Mony and writhing like a viper. The triple spasm was simultaneous. The trio parted company and the general, immediately on his feet, brandished his sabre shouting:

--- Now, Prince Vibescu, you must die, you've seen too much!

But Mony disarmed him without difficulty.

He then bound him hand and foot and laid him in a corner of

the wagon near the corpse of the little Chinese. After which he continued till dawn his delightful fuckings with the general's wife. When he left her she was tired out and asleep. The general slept too, feet and wrists tied.

Mony went to Fédor's tent: there too they had been fucking all night long. Alexine, Culculine, Fédor and Cornaboeux were sleeping naked, sprawled in a heap on some greatcoats. Spunk was sticking to the women's short-hairs and the men's pricks dangled lamentably.

Mony let them sleep on and began to wander through the camp. An imminent engagement with the Japanese was being proclaimed. The soldiers were seeing to kit or having breakfast. Cavalrymen were grooming their horses.

A Cossack whose hands were cold was busily warming them in the tired old cunt of his mare. The beast was whinnying softly; all of a sudden, the reheated cossack heaved himself onto a chair behind his nag and, hoisting out a prick as vast as a spear shaft jabbed it delightedly into the animal vulva which was exuding a most aphrodisiac equine elixir, since the human brute discharged thrice with great thrusts of arse before decunting.

An officer who observed this act of bestiality approached the soldier with Mony. He reproached him smartly for having surrendered to his passion:

--- My friend, he said to him, masturbation is a military virtue.

Every good soldier should know that in time of war onanism is the only amorous act permitted. Toss off, but touch neither women nor beasts.

Besides, masturbation is most laudable, in that it allows men and women to accustom themselves to their impending and ultimate separation. The morals, minds, clothes and tastes of the two sexes differ more and more. It's high time that was realized, and it seems to me essential, if one wishes to rule the earth, that one come to grips with this natural law which will soon be imperative.

The officer moved off, leaving a pensive Mony to regain Fédor's tent.

Suddenly the prince was aware of an outlandish clamour, akin to that of Irish mourners keening over some stranger's death.

As he drew nearer to it the noise changed, taking on a rhythm via sharp tapping sounds as if a mad conductor were rapping his baton on his rostrum while the orchestra played muted.

The prince ran faster and a strange spectacle met his eyes. A troop of soldiers commanded by an officer was taking turns whipping, with long flexible canes, the backs of convicted men stripped to the waist.

Mony, who out-ranked the man in charge of the floggers, wanted to take over command.

A new culprit was led along. He was a handsome Tartar lad who spoke hardly any Russian. The prince made him strip stark naked, then the soldiers thrashed him, so that the morning chill might bite him at the same time as the rods cut into him.

He was impassive and this calmness irritated Mony; he had a quiet word with the officer who soon brought back a serving-girl from the brasserie. She was a buxom kellnerine whose rump and chest indecently filled the uniform buttoning her up tight. This fine and substantial girl arrived constricted by her outfit and waddling like a duck.

--- You're indecent, my girl, Mony told her. A woman such as you does not dress like a man; one hundred strokes of the cane to teach you that.

The unhappy girl trembled all over but, at a motion from Mony, the soldiers stripped her.

Her nudity contrasted singularly with that of the Tartar.

He was very lanky, with an emaciated face and small, sly, untroubled eyes; his limbs had that thinness ascribed to John the Baptist after he had lived for some time on locusts. His arms, chest and skinny legs were hairy, his circumcised penis was acquiring firmness because of the fustigation and its glans was purple, colour of a drunkard's vomit.

The kellnerine, a fine specimen of the Germanic female from Brunswick, was heavy in the rump; akin to a sturdy Luxembourg mare let loose among the stallions. Her flaxen hair rendered her quite poetical and the Rhenish Nixies must not have been dissimilar.

Very pale blonde short-hairs hung down right between her thighs. This shaggy shock completely covered a prominent mound. The woman radiated good health and all the soldiers felt their virile members spontaneously present arms.

Mony requested a knout and one was brought him.

--- Provost filth, he shouted at him, if you want to save your own skin, don't spare this whore's.

Without reply, the Tartar like a connoisseur examined the instrument of torture composed of leather thongs studded with iron filings.

The woman was sobbing and begging for mercy in German. Her pink and white body was trembling. Mony made her kneel, then, with one kick, forced her fat arse to stick out. The Tartar first shook the knout in the air, then, vigorously raising his arm, was about to strike when the unfortunate kellnerine who was quaking in every limb let fly a sonorous fart that made all the spectators laugh, including the Tartar himself, who dropped the knout. Mony, cane in hand, struck him across the face, telling him:

--- Idiot, I said thrash her, not laugh.

Then he gave him the cane, ordering him to beat the German woman with that first to get her used to it. The Tartar began to strike with regularity. His member, straight behind the victim's fat arse, stood stiff but, despite his concupiscence, his arm rose and fell rhythmically, the cane was very flexible, each blow whistled through the air then came down smartly across the taut skin on which the stripes showed.

The Tartar was an artist and the blows he was inflicting were joining up to form a calligraphic design.

On the base of the back, above the buttocks, there soon appeared distinctly the word *whore*.

He was vigorously applauded while the cries of the German woman became ever more raucous. Her arse with each blow of the cane would writhe momentarily then lift, the clenched buttocks would immediately slacken; it was then possible to catch sight of the arsehole and the cunt below it, yawning and wet.

Gradually, she seemed to get used to the blows. At each thwack of the cane, her back would rise feebly, the arse would half open and the cunt part pleasurably as if some unexpected enjoyment had come to possess her.

She soon fell as though choked with pleasure and Mony just then stayed the Tartar's hand.

He gave him back the knout and the man, crazed with desire, started hitting the German woman's back with this cruel weapon. Every blow left several deep and bleeding marks for, instead of raising aloft the knout after each stroke, the Tartar would tug it towards him so that the iron filings affixed to the thongs bore away shreds of skin and flesh which fell right and left, spattering the uniforms of the soldiery with droplets of blood.

The German woman no longer felt the pain, she writhed, twisted and hissed with pleasure. Her face was red, she was drooling and when Mony ordered the Tartar to stop, the traces of the word *whore* had disappeared, for her back was nothing but an open wound.

The Tartar remained standing, bloody knout in hand; he seemed to be asking for approval, but Mony gave him a scornful glance:

--- You started off well, but you finished badly. Such work is execrable. You lashed out like an ignoramus. Soldiers, take away this woman and bring one of her companions to me, into this tent here: it's empty. I'm going to see to this miserable Tartar.

He dismissed the soldiers, several of whom carried away the German woman, and the prince with his convicted man went into the tent.

He began beating him with all his might, with two canes. The Tartar, excited by the spectacle he had just witnessed and in which he had been the protagonist, did not long restrain the sperm seething in his balls. His member stiffened under Mony's blows, and the spunk that spurted bedaubed the canvas of the tent.

At this moment, another woman was brought in. She was in her nightgown for they had surprised her in bed. Her features expressed stupefaction and profound terror. She was dumb, and hoarse inarticulate sounds were issuing from her throat.

She was a beautiful girl, a native of Sweden. Daughter to the director of the brasserie, she had married a Dane, her father's partner. She had given birth four months before and was feeding the child herself. She was aged about twenty four. Her breasts swollen with milk – for she was a good wet-nurse – filled out the nightgown.

Immediately Mony saw her, he dismissed the soldiers who had brought her and he lifted up her gown. The Swede's large thighs resembled column shafts and were supporting a superb edifice; her bush was golden and nicely curled. Mony ordered the Tartar to scourge her while he himself tongued her. Blows rained down on the arms of the beautiful mute, but the prince's mouth down below was gleaning the amorous liquor distilled by this boreal cunt.

Next, he lay down naked on the bed, having removed her nightgown; the woman was on heat. She placed herself atop him and his prick entered deep between thighs of a dazzling whiteness. Her firm and massive arse rose and fell rhythmically. The prince took one breast in his mouth and began sucking a delicious milk.

The Tartar remained by no means inactive, but, making the cane swish, he administered stinging blows on the hemispheres of the mute, whose climax he expedited. He lashed her like a lunatic, welting that sublime arse, striping regardless the fine plump white shoulders, leaving furrows on the back. Mony, who had shagged a good deal already, took a long time coming, and the mute, excited by the rod, came fifteen times, during his one fuck.

Then he got to his feet and, seeing the Tartar in a fine state of erection, ordered him to fuck the beauteous wet-nurse dog-fashion as she still did not seem sated; he himself taking the knout, he bloodied the back of the soldier who came emitting terrible shrieks.

The Tartar did not leave his post. Stoically enduring the blows dealt by the terrible knout, he ransacked without respite the amorous redoubt wherein he was ensconced. Five times he there deposited his ardent offering. Then he lay motionless on the woman, who was still wracked with pleasurable spasms.

But the prince abused him, he had lit a cigarette and burned the Tartar's shoulders in several places. Then he stuck a lighted match under his balls and the burn had the effect of reviving the indefatigable member. The Tartar rode off once more towards a new discharge. Mony took up the knout again and with all his might flailed at the united bodies of the Tartar and the mute; blood spurted, the blows fell with crisp smacks. Mony was swearing in French, Romanian and Russian. The Tartar was dreadfully stimulated, but a look of hatred for Mony flashed into his eyes. He knew sign-language and, passing his hand over his partner's face, he made signs for her which the latter understood admirably.

Towards the end of this fucking bout, Mony had a new whim: he applied his glowing cigarette to one of the mute's wet nipples. The milk, a droplet of which was beading on the elongated tit, extinguished the cigarette, but the woman uttered a bellow of terror as she came.

She made a sign for the Tartar who decunted immediately. Both of them flung themselves on Mony and disarmed him. The woman took one cane and the Tartar the knout. Their eyes full of hatred, and stirred by the hope of vengeance, they began cruelly whipping the officer who had made them suffer. Mony cried out and struggled in vain; the blows spared no part of his body. The Tartar, though, fearing that his vengeance upon an officer might have disastrous consequences, soon hurled away his knout, contenting himself like the woman with a simple cane. Mony was jumping about under the thrashing and the woman persisted in belabouring the belly, balls and prick of the prince.

During this time, the Dane, the mute's husband, had noticed her disappearance, for the little girl was wailing for her mother's breast. He took the infant in his arms and went in search of his wife.·

A soldier pointed out the tent where she was, but omitted to tell him what she was doing there. Crazed with jealousy, the Dane rushed forward, lifted the flap and entered the tent. The spectacle was not exactly commonplace: his wife, naked and bloody in the company of a naked and bleeding Tartar, was whipping a young man.

The knout was on the ground, the Dane laid down his child, took up the knout and with it lashed out as hard as he could at his wife and the Tartar who both fell to the ground screaming with pain.

Under the blows Mony's member had again erected, grown stiff while he was contemplating this conjugal scene.

The little girl was crying on the ground. Mony seized and unswaddled her, kissed her diminutive pink arse and small chubby hairless slit, then, applying the latter to his prick and covering her mouth with one hand, he violated her; his member tore this infantile flesh. Mony did not take long to come. He was discharging when the father and mother, too late noticing the crime, flung themselves upon him.

The mother picked up the child. The Tartar hastily dressed and made himself scarce; but the Dane, eyes bloodshot, raised the knout. He was about to deal Mony's head a deadly blow when he caught sight of an officer's uniform on the ground. His arm fell to his side again, for he knew that a Russian officer is inviolable, he may rape or plunder but the sutler who dared raise a hand against him would be hanged on the spot.

Mony understood all that was passing through the Dane's mind. He took advantage of it, getting up and quickly seizing his revolver. With a scornful look, he ordered the Dane to take off his trousers. Then, revolver levelled, he ordered the Dane to bugger his daughter. In vain did the Dane beg, he had to introduce his paltry member into the tender bottom of the unconscious nurseling.

And during this time Mony, armed with a cane and holding his revolver in his left hand, was raining blows on the back of the mute, who was sobbing and writhing with pain. The cane was striking once more at flesh swollen from the previous blows and the pain endured by the poor woman made for a horrible spectacle. Mony bore it with admirable courage and his arm remained steadfast in its fustigation until the moment the hapless father had discharged into the arse of his little daughter.

Mony dressed then and ordered the Danish woman to do likewise. Then he pleasantly assisted the couple in reviving the child.

--- Heartless woman, he said to the mute, your child wants to suck, can't you see that?

The Dane made signs to his wife who, chastely, brought out her breast and gave suck to the infant.

--- As for you, said Mony to the Dane, take care. You violated your daughter in front of me. I can destroy you. So be discreet, my word will always prevail against yours. Go in peace. Your business henceforth depends on my goodwill. If you are discreet, I'll protect you, but if you tell what happened here you will be hanged.

The Dane kissed the hand of the dashing officer, shedding tears of gratitude, and rapidly led his wife and child away. Mony set off for Fédor's tent.

The sleepers had awoken and had dressed after their ablutions.

Throughout the day, there were preparations for battle, which commenced that evening. Mony, Cornaboeux and the two women closeted themselves inside Fédor's tent while he went off to fight at the outposts. Soon the first cannonades were heard and stretcher-bearers returned carrying the wounded.

The tent was converted into a casualty station. Cornaboeux and the two women were conscripted to collect up the dying. Mony remained alone with three wounded Russian soldiers who were delirious.

Then there arrived a lady from the Red Cross clad in an elegant écru overcoat with badge on the right arm.

She was an extremely pretty woman from the Polish aristocracy. She had a voice sweet as an angel's and when the wounded heard it they turned their dying eyes towards her believing they were seeing the madonna.

She gave Mony curt orders in her sweet voice. He would obey like a child, astonished by this pretty girl's energy and by the strange glow which now and then emanated from her green eyes.

From time to time her seraphic face would grow hard and a cloud of unforgivable vices seemed to darken her brow. It was apparent that this woman's innocence had criminal intermissions.

Mony observed her; he soon noticed that her fingers were lingering longer than necessary in the wounds.

They brought in a wounded man horrible to behold. His face was bloody and his chest split open.

The nurse dressed him with voluptuous delight. She had put her right hand into the gaping cavity and seemed to enjoy the contact of the quivering flesh.

All of a sudden the ghoul raised her eyes and saw opposite her, the other side of the stretcher, Mony, who was gazing at her with a disdainful smile.

She blushed, but he reassured her:

--- Calm yourself, don't be alarmed, I understand better than anyone the sensual pleasure you can experience. I myself have tainted hands. Take your pleasure with these wounded men, but don't you refuse my embraces.

She lowered her eyes in silence. Mony was soon behind her. He lifted her skirts and uncovered a marvellous arse whose buttocks were so tightly clenched that they seemed to have sworn never to part.

She was now, with an angelic smile on her lips, feverishly tearing at the dying man's dreadful wound. She bent forward to allow Mony fuller enjoyment of the sight of her arse.

He then introduced his shaft between the satin lips of her cunt, back-scuttling her, and with his right hand caressed her buttocks while the left went ferreting for the clitoris under the petticoats. The nurse came silently, her hands clutching inside the wound of the dying man who emitted a hideous death-rattle. He expired exactly as Mony discharged. The nurse at once ejected Mony and, removing the breeches of the dead man, whose member had an iron rigidity, she plunged it into her cunt, still taking her pleasure silently, and with her face more angelic than ever.

Mony first spanked this fat arse which was swinging about and whose cunt-lips were puking out and quickly re-ingesting the cadaveric column. His prick soon regained its initial stiffness and, placing himself behind the nurse, who was coming, he buggered her like a madman.

Afterwards they readjusted their clothing and a handsome young man was brought in whose arms and legs had been torn away by grapeshot. This human trunk still possessed a fine member whose firmness was ideal. The nurse, as soon as she was alone with Mony, sat herself on the prick of the trunk who was wheezing his last throes, and during this breathless ride she sucked Mony's prick which soon spent like a carmelite. The trunk-man had not yet died; he was bleeding copiously from the stumps of all four limbs. The ghoul sucked his prick and brought him death through this horrible caress. The sperm that came from this cocksucking, she confessed to Mony, was almost cold and she seemed so excited that Mony, who felt exhausted, begged her to undo her dress. He sucked her tits, then she knelt down and tried to revive the princely prick by masturbating it between her paps.

--- Alas! cried Mony, cruel woman whose God-given mission it is to finish off the wounded, who are you? who are you?

--- I am, she said, the daughter of Jan Morneski, the revolutionary prince whom the infamous Gurko sent to his death at Tobolsk.

To avenge myself and to avenge Poland my motherland I dispatch Russian soldiers. I would like to kill Kouropatkin and I pray for the deaths of the Romanovs.

My brother, who is also my lover and who deflowered me during a pogrom in Warsaw, lest my virginity fell prey to a Cossack, shares the selfsame sentiments as I. He misled the regiment he was commanding and had it drown in Lake Baikal. He had informed me of his intention before his departure.

Thus it is that we Poles wreak our vengeance on Muscovite tyranny.

These patriotic frenzies have worked upon my senses, and my most noble passions have given way to those of cruelty. I am cruel, you see, like Tamerlane, Attila and Ivan the Terrible. I once used to be pious as a saint. Today, Messalina and Catherine would be mere lambs compared to me.

It was not without a shudder that Mony heard the declarations of this exquisite whore. He wanted at all costs to lick her arse in honour of Poland, and told her how he had been indirectly involved in the conspiracy that led to the death of Alexander Obrenovitch, in Belgrade.

She listened to him in admiration.

--- Ah to see the day, she burst out, the Tsar's flung out of the window!

Mony being a loyal officer protested against this defenestration and avowed his allegiance to legitimate autocracy:

--- I admire you, he said to the Polish woman, but if I were the

Tsar I'd destroy all the Poles outright. Those inept drunkards never stop fabricating bombs and making the planet uninhabitable. Even in Paris, those sadistic types, who belong under the jurisdiction of the Court of Assizes as much as to the Salpêtrière, worry the life out of peaceable citizens.[28]

--- It's true, said the Polish woman, that my compatriots are none too frolicsome, but only return them their homeland, let them speak their native tongue, and Poland will again become the country of chivalric honour, of luxury and pretty women.

--- You are right! cried Mony and, pushing the nurse onto a stretcher, he tromboned her in leisurely posture as, fucking all the while, they chatted of odd veneries and arcane topics. One might have deemed it a *Decameron* and themselves surrounded by the victims of plague.[29]

--- Fascinating woman, said Mony, let us plight our troth with our souls!

--- Yes, she said, we shall be married after the war and noise abroad our cruelties everywhere.

--- It suits me, said Mony, but let them be legal cruelties.

--- Perhaps you're right, said the nurse, there's nothing so sweet as accomplishing whatever is permitted.

They thereupon went into a trance, clasping and biting one another and coming intensely.

At that moment cries were heard; the Russian army in disarray was letting itself be overrun by the Japanese troops.

The horrible screams of the wounded were audible, the din of artillery, the ominous rumble of ammunition waggons and the prolonged crackle of rifle fire.

The tent was opened abruptly and a troop of Japanese invaded it. Mony and the nurse barely had time to readjust their clothing.

A Japanese officer advanced towards Prince Vibescu.

--- You are my prisoner, he told him, but with a single revolver shot Mony killed him on the spot, then, in full view of the stupefied Japanese, he broke his sword across his knee.

96

Another Japanese officer came forward at that, and the soldiers surrounded Mony who accepted being taken prisoner, and when he emerged from the tent accompanied by the little Nipponese officer, he could see in the distance along the plain the tardy stragglers who were painfully attempting to rejoin the routed Russian army.

Chapter Eight

A prisoner on parole, Mony was free to come and go in the Japanese camp. He searched in vain for Cornaboeux. In his comings and goings he noticed that he was being observed by the officer who had taken him prisoner. He wanted to befriend him and managed to strike up a friendship with him. This Shintoist was quite a sensualist who told him wonderful things about the wife he had left in Japan.

--- She is funny and charming, he would say, and I adore her as I adore the Trinity Ame-no-Minakanushi-no-Kami. She is fertile as Izanagi and Izanami, creators of the earth and begetters of men, and beautiful as Ama-Terasu, daughter of these gods, and the sun itself. While she waits for me she is thinking of me and plucking the thirteen strings of her *koto* made from imperial paulownia wood or playing upon her seventeen-pipe *sio*.[30]

--- And you, asked Mony, have you never felt like fucking since you've been in the war?

--- As for myself, said the officer, when the urge becomes too much for me, I toss off while looking at obscene pictures! And he showed Mony little books full of woodcuts of an astonishing obscenity. One of these books depicted women making love with all sorts of animals, cats, birds, tigers, dogs, fish and even octopi which hideously entwined their sucker-studded tentacles around the bodies of the hysterical strumpets.

99

--- All our officers and men, said the officer, have books of this kind. They can do without women and toss off while looking at these priapic drawings.

Mony often went and visited the wounded Russians. There he again met the Polish nurse who in Fédor's tent had given him lessons in cruelty.

Among the wounded was a captain who came from Archangel. His wound was not especially serious and Mony often used to converse with him, seated at his bedside.

One day the wounded man, whose name was Katache, handed Mony a letter, begging him to read it. The letter had it that Katache's wife was deceiving him with a fur-trader.

--- I adore her, said the captain, I love this woman more than myself and I suffer terribly knowing she is with another man, yet I am happy, dreadfully happy.

--- How do you reconcile these two emotions? asked Mony. They are contradictory.

--- They're mixed up inside me, said Katache, and I can't conceive of pleasure at all without pain.

--- So you're a masochist? enquired Mony, distinctly curious.

--- If you wish! the officer acquiesced, but masochism anyhow conforms to the precepts of the Christian religion. Look, since you're interested in me, I'm going to tell you my story.

--- I'd like that, said Mony with alacrity, but first drink this lemonade to cool your gullet.

Captain Katache began thus:

--- I was born in 1874 in Archangel, and from my earliest years I would experience a bitter joy every time I was punished. The various mishaps which befell my family heightened this faculty of taking pleasure in misfortune and sharpened it.

Certainly that came of being too tender-hearted. My father was assassinated and I recall, I was fifteen at the time, that due to his decease I experienced my first ejaculation. The sheer shock and fright made me discharge. My mother went mad, and when I'd go and visit her in the asylum I'd toss off while listening to her rant and rave in her vile way, for she believed she'd been turned into a latrine, monsieur, and she would describe imaginary arses that shat in her. She had to be locked up the day she supposed the trench was full. She became dangerous and used to yell loudly for the cesspit emptiers to drain her. I'd listen to her with distress. She would recognize me.

--- My son, she'd say, you don't love your mother any more, you visit other privies. Sit on me and shit in comfort.

Where better to shit than in one's mother's breast?

And, son, don't forget, the hole's full. Yesterday a publican who came and shat in me had an attack of colic. I'm overflowing, I can't take any more. You absolutely must fetch the sewermen.

Believe me, monsieur, I was profoundly disgusted and distressed too, for I adored my mother, but at the same time I felt an unspeakable pleasure on hearing these vile utterances. Yes, monsieur, I enjoyed it and I used to toss myself off.

I was shoved into the army and was able, thanks to my connections, to remain in the North. I saw a great deal of the family of a Protestant pastor who'd settled in Archangel; he was English and had a daughter so splendid that no descriptions of mine could portray for you even a fraction of the beauty that was hers in reality. One day we were dancing together during a private family function, and after the waltz, as if by accident, Florence laid her hand between my thighs and asked:

--- Have you gone stiff?

She noticed that I had a raging erection; but she smiled and said to me:

--- And I'm all wet too, but not in your honour. I've come because of Dyre.

And she went fondly over to Dyre Kissird who was a Norwegian commercial traveller. They joked awhile, then the band struck up another dance and they set off in each other's arms, looking at one another amorously. I suffered martyrdom. Jealousy gnawed at my heart. And if Florence was desirable, I desired her even more from the day I knew she did not love me. I discharged while watching her dance with my rival. I imagined them at it in each other's arms and I had to turn away so no one saw my tears.

Then, driven by the demon of lust and jealousy, I swore to myself that I would make her my wife. She's a strange girl, is Florence, she speaks four languages: French, German, Russian and English, but she doesn't really know any of them, and the lingo she uses has a barbarous flavour. I myself speak very good French and I'm thoroughly familiar with French literature, especially the late nineteenth century poets. I would write Florence verses I called symbolist and which simply reflected my misery.

The anemone flowered in the name of Archangel
When angels would weep at being chilblained.
And the name of Florence with sighs had maintained
Heady vows on the port steps as barometers fell.

White voices singing in the name of Archangel
Often trilled neniae on Florence
Whose flowers, returning, plastered in heavy trance
Thaw-sweaty ceiling and exudative wall.

   O Florence! Archangel!

The one: bay berry, but the other: herb angelic,
Women take turns, leaning over the lip of the well
And shower into its blackness flower or relic,
Archangel relics and flowers of Archangel![31]

Garrison life in northern Russia in peacetime has many spare-time activities. Hunting and social obligations there take up much of the military man's life. Hunting held few attractions for me and my social activities were summed up more or less thus: to win Florence whom I loved and who did not love me. This was a hard task. I died a thousand deaths since Florence despised me more and more, she would make fun of me and would flirt with polar bear hunters or Scandinavian traders. One day, when a wretched French operetta company had ventured into our remote mists to give some performances, I even surprised Florence during an aurora borealis skating hand in hand with the tenor, a repulsive billy-goat born in Carcassonne.

But I was rich, monsieur, and, Florence's father not being indifferent to my suit, I finally married her.

We left for France and on the way she never even let me kiss her. We arrived in Nice in February, during the carnival.

We rented a villa and one day during the battle of flowers, Florence notified me that she had decided to lose her virginity that very evening. I thought that my love was about to be rewarded. Alas! my voluptuous calvary was just beginning.

Florence added that it was not I whom she had selected to fulfil this function.

--- You are too ridiculous, said she, and you wouldn't know how. I want a Frenchman, the French are lovers and they're experts at that. I myself shall choose my dream reamer during the festival.

Accustomed to obedience, I bowed my head. We went to the battle of flowers. A young man with a Nice or Monegasque accent looked at Florence. She looked back, smiling. I was suffering more than they suffer in any of the circles of Dante's hell.

During the battle of flowers we saw him again. He was alone in a carriage adorned with a profusion of unusual flowers. We were in a victoria that was enough to drive one mad, for Florence had wanted it decorated entirely with tuberoses.

Whenever the young man's carriage met up with ours, he threw flowers at Florence who would ogle him amorously, throwing bouquets of tuberoses at him.

On one circuit, irritated, she flung her bouquet very hard, and its limp and viscous flowers and stems left a stain on the fop's flannel togs. Immediately Florence apologized and, promptly alighting, she climbed into the young man's carriage.

He was a rich Niçois comfortably off from the olive oil business left him by his father.

Prospero, that was the youth's name, welcomed my wife without more ado and at the end of the battle, his carriage won first prize and mine second. The band was playing. I saw my wife holding the banner won by my rival whom she was kissing passionately.

That evening, she insisted on dining with me and Prospero, whom she brought to our villa. It was a beautiful night and I was in agony.

My wife made the pair of us enter the bedroom, I wretchedly depressed and Prospero quite astounded and somewhat embarrassed at his good fortune.

She pointed to an armchair and told me:

--- You're going to watch a lesson in lust, try to gain something from it.

Then she told Prospero to undress her; this he did with some grace.

Florence was charming. Her firm flesh, plumper than one would have supposed, palpitated at the touch of the Niçois. He too undressed and his member was erect. I noted with pleasure that it was no bigger than mine. It was actually smaller and pointed. All things considered, it was a fitting fit for a maidenhead. Both of them were charming; she with her hair elegantly done, eyes sparkling with desire, and pink in her lace chemise.

Prospero sucked her breasts, which jutted like cooing doves and, slipping his hand under the chemise, he manipulated her a little while she amused herself by pulling down his prick then letting go so it would slap back against his belly. I was weeping in my armchair. Suddenly Prospero took my wife in his arms and raised her chemise at the back; her sweet chubby arse appeared, dimples everywhere.

Prospero spanked her while she was laughing, that behind of hers came up roses mingled with lilies. She soon turned serious, saying:

--- Take me.

He carried her to the bed and I heard the cry of pain my wife uttered when the torn hymen left the way open to the conqueror's cock.

To me they paid no more heed, I who was sobbing, yet revelling in my misery, as, unable to restrain myself, I pulled out my cock and tossed off in their honour.

They fucked away ten times or so. Then my wife, as if just noticing my presence, said to me:

--- Come and see, dear husband, what a fine job Prospero has done.

I approached the bed, prick to the fore, and my wife, seeing that my member was bigger than Prospero's, became greatly contemptuous of him. She frigged me, saying:

--- Prospero, your prick's no good, for my husband's a halfwit and his is much bigger than yours. You've deceived me. My husband's going to avenge me. 'André' – that's my name – 'whip this man till you draw blood'.

I hurled myself upon him and seizing a dog-whip that was on the bedside table, I flogged him with all the strength my jealousy lent me. I whipped him a long time. I was stronger than he and in the end my wife took pity on him. She made him get dressed and sent him packing with an emphatic farewell.

When he had gone, I thought my sorrows were at an end. Alas! She said to me:

--- André, give me your prick.

She frigged me but did not let me touch her. Then she called her dog, a handsome great dane, which she wanked for a while. When its pointed prick was erect, she got the dog to mount her, ordering me to help the beast, whose tongue hung out as it panted with lust.

I was in such distress that I fainted as I ejaculated. When I was myself again, Florence was calling me with loud screams. The dog's penis, once in, would not come out again. Both of them, woman and beast, had spent half an hour making fruitless efforts to separate. A nodosity was snagging the great dane's prick within my wife's clenched vagina. I had recourse to cold water which soon restored them to liberty. My wife since that day had no more desire to make love with dogs. To reward me, she tossed me off and then sent me away to sleep in my own room.

The next evening I begged my wife to allow me to fulfil my marital rights.

--- I adore you, I was saying, nobody loves you as I do, I am your slave. Do with me what you will.

She was naked and delectable. Her hair was spread out across the bed, her strawberry nipples attracted me and I wept. She took out my prick and slowly, with little tugs, tossed me off. Then she rang the bell, and a young chambermaid she had engaged in Nice entered, in a nightgown for she had been in bed. My wife made me take my place in the armchair again and I witnessed the revels of the two tribades who indulged themselves feverishly, panting and slobbering. They gamahuched, rubbed off on each other's thighs, and I watched young Ninette's large and solid arse heave above my wife whose eyes were drowning in lust.

I wanted to have them both, but Florence and Ninette laughed at me and tossed me off, then immersed themselves once more in their unnatural lusts.

The next day, my wife did not call upon Ninette, but it was an officer in the *Chasseurs Alpins* who was to cause me grief. His member was enormous and darkish. He was coarse, and insulted and beat me.

When he had fucked my wife, he ordered me to come close to the bed and, taking up the dog-whip, he struck me across the face. I let out a cry of pain. Alas! a burst of laughter from my wife revived in me that bitter-sweet pleasure I had previously experienced.

I let myself be undressed by the cruel soldier, who needed to whip so as to excite himself.

When I was naked, the *Chasseur Alpin* insulted me, he called me: *cuckold, wittol, horned fool,* and, raising the whip, he brought it down on my backside. The first blows were cruel, but I saw that my wife had a taste for my suffering, her pleasure becoming mine. I myself did derive pleasure from suffering.

Each blow was falling upon me like a rather violent spasm of pleasure on my buttocks. The first smarting pain immediately turned into an exquisite tickling and I got a hard-on. The blows had soon ripped my skin, and the blood flowing from my buttocks had strangely stimulated me. It greatly increased my pleasure.

My wife's finger was working in the moss that adorned her pretty cunt. With her other hand she was frigging my torturer. The blows suddenly redoubled and I felt that the moment of crisis was approaching for me. My brain reeled with bliss; the martyrs honoured by the Church must have had such moments.

I rose to my feet, bleeding and stiff of prick, and flung myself on my wife.

Neither she nor her lover could stop me. I fell into the arms of my spouse and no sooner had my member touched the adored short-hairs of her cunt than I discharged uttering horrible shrieks.

But the Alpinist at once hauled me from my post; my wife, red with rage, said I must be punished.

She took hairpins and stuck them into my body, one by one, voluptuously. I uttered dreadful cries of pain. Any man would have had pity on me. But my unworthy wife lay on the red bed and, legs spread, pulled her lover to her by his enormous donkey prong, then, parting the lips and short-hairs of her cunt, she forced his member in up to the balls, while her lover bit her breasts and I rolled around like a madman on the floor, making the painful pins sink in ever deeper.

I awoke in the arms of pretty Ninette who, crouched over me, was extracting the pins. I listened to my wife in the next room swear and cry out as she came in the officer's arms. The pain of the pins Ninette was extracting from me, with that being caused me by my wife's crisis, gave me an appalling cockstand.

Ninette, as I've said, was crouched over me, I seized her by the merkin and felt her moist slit beneath my finger.

But alas! at that moment the door opened and a horrible *botcha*, meaning a Piedmontese builder's labourer, came in.

It was Ninette's lover and he flew into a wild rage. He lifted his mistress's skirts and began spanking her in front of me. Then he took off his leather belt and thrashed her with that. She was crying out:

--- I didn't make love with the master!

--- Which is why, said the hodman, he had you by the arse-hairs.

Ninette defended herself in vain. Her brunette's broad beam jolted about under the blows of the thong which hissed and sliced through the air like a striking snake. Her backside was soon on fire. She clearly liked such punishments for she turned round and, grasping her lover by the flies, undid his breeches to fetch out a prick and balls that together must have weighed a good three and a half kilos.

The swine was stiff as a skunk. He lay on top of Ninette who crossed her slim and wiry legs around the workman's back. I saw the great member enter a hairy cunt that swallowed it like a pellet and puked it back out like a piston. They were a long time coming and their cries mingled with those of my wife.

When they had done, the ginger-haired *botcha* stood up and, seeing that I was wanking, insulted me, picked up his belt again, and thrashed me all over. The thong caused me terrible pain, for I was weakened and no longer had strength to feel lustful pleasure. The buckle bit cruelly into my flesh. I was screaming:

--- Mercy!...

But just then my wife came in with her lover and, since there was a barrel-organ playing under our windows, the two unbridled couples began dancing on my body, crushing my balls and nose and making me bleed profusely.

I fell ill. But I had my revenge too, because the *botcha* fell off some scaffolding and broke his skull and the Alpine officer, having insulted one of his comrades, was killed by him in a duel.

An order from His Majesty called me to serve in the Far East and I've left my wife who's deceiving me still...

Thus did Katache finish his narrative. It had inflamed Mony and the Polish nurse, who had entered towards the end of the story and listened quivering with repressed lust.

The prince and the nurse flung themselves on the hapless injured man, uncovered him and, seizing some Russian flagstaffs captured in the last battle and now strewn about the floor, they began beating the wretched man, whose backside jerked at every blow. He was crying out in delirium:

--- O my sweet Florence, is that your divine hand beating me once more? You're making me hard... Every blow makes me come... Don't forget to toss me off... Oh! that's good. You're hitting my shoulders too hard. Oh! that blow drew blood... It's flowing for you... my wife... my turtle dove... my dear little teaser...

The whore of a nurse was thumping him like nobody's business. The wretch's arse rose up livid and bespattered in places with a pale blood. Mony's heart sank, he was aware of his own cruelty, and his fury turned against the infamous nurse. He hoisted her skirts and started hitting her. She fell to the ground, wriggling that rotten rump of hers enhanced by a beauty spot.

He struck her with all his might, drawing blood across the satin flesh.

She rolled over shrieking like a maniac. Mony's stick then caught her on the belly with a resounding thwack.

He had a sudden inspiration and, retrieving the other stick

which the nurse had dropped, he took to playing drumrolls on the Polish woman's naked belly. *Flam* turned into *rat-tat-tat* with dizzying rapidity, and little Bara, of glorious memory, hardly drummed so fine a charge upon the bridge at Arcola.[32]

Finally the stomach split open; Mony kept on drumming at it and, outside the infirmary the Japanese soldiers, thinking it was a call to arms, were reassembling. The bugles sounded the alert within the camp. On all sides, regiments were lining up, and it was lucky for them that they did, for the Russians had just assumed the offensive and were advancing towards the Japanese camp. Had it not been for the drumming of Prince Mony Vibescu, the Japanese camp would have been taken. This was, furthermore, the decisive victory of the Nipponese. It was due to a Romanian sadist.

Suddenly some medical orderlies came into the ward carrying wounded. They caught sight of the prince beating upon the Polish woman's burst belly. They saw the injured man naked and bloody on his bed.

They threw themselves on the prince, bound him and led him away.

A court-martial sentenced him to death by flagellation and nothing could make the Japanese judges relent. An appeal to the Mikado for clemency had no success.

Prince Vibescu bravely resigned himself to his fate and prepared to die like a true hereditary Hospodar of Romania.

Chapter Nine

The day of the execution arrived; Prince Vibescu confessed, communicated, made his will and wrote to his parents. Then a young girl of twelve was led into his prison cell. This astonished him, but seeing that he was being left to himself, he began to paw her.

She was charming and told him in Romanian that she was from Bucharest and had been taken prisoner by the Japanese among the rearguard of the Russian army to which her parents were sutlers.

She had been asked whether she wished to lose her virginity to a Romanian sentenced to death and she had consented.

Mony lifted her skirts and sucked her plump little cunt as yet devoid of hair, then he spanked her gently while she was wanking him. Next he put the knob of his prick between the little Romanian's childish legs, but could not gain admittance. She assisted him in all his efforts, by bucking her arse and offering her small breasts round as tangerines to the prince to kiss. He flew into an erotic frenzy and his prick at last penetrated the girl, finally ravishing her maidenhead, making the innocent blood flow.

Then Mony stood up and, since he had nothing more to hope for from human justice, he strangled the little girl after gouging out her eyes, while she uttered frightful cries.

The Japanese soldiers then entered and marched him out. A

herald read the sentence in the courtyard of the prison, which was an ancient Chinese pagoda of amazing architecture.

The sentence was brief: the condemned man was to receive one stroke of the rod from each man in the Japanese army thereon encamped. This army comprised eleven thousand elements.

And while the herald read out the sentence, the prince recollected his hectic life. The women of Bucharest, the Serbian vice-consul, Paris, the slaughter in the sleeping-car, the little Japanese at Port Arthur, all of it reeled through his memory.

One fact became clear. He remembered the boulevard Malesherbes; Culculine in a spring frock was sauntering along towards the Madeleine and he, Mony, was saying to her:

--- If I don't make love twenty times running, may the eleven thousand virgins or even eleven thousand rods chastise me.

He had not fucked twenty times in a row, and the day had arrived when eleven thousand rods were going to chastise him.

He was there still in dream when the soldiers shook him and led him before his executioners.

The eleven thousand Japanese were ranged in two rows facing each other. Each man held a flexible cane. Mony was stripped, then he had to march down this cruel road bordered by torturers. The first blows merely made him flinch. They fell upon a skin of satin and left dark red marks. He bore the first thousand strokes stoically, then fell in his own blood, prick erect.

He was then put onto a barrow and the doleful promenade continued, punctuated by the sharp slaps of canes biting into swollen and bleeding flesh. Soon his prick could no longer retain its jet of sperm and, jerking upward several times, it spat its whitish liquid into the faces of the soldiers, who beat this tattered relic of humanity harder still.

At the two thousandth blow, Mony gave up the ghost. The sun was dazzling. The songs of the Manchurian birds made the spring morning even more bright and gay. The full sentence was executed and the last soldiers delivered their single cane-stroke upon a shapeless mass, a sort of raw sausagemeat, none of it any longer recognizable save for the face, which had been sedulously respected and wherein the glassy eyes staring wide seemed to contemplate divine majesty in the world beyond.

At that moment a convoy of Russian prisoners passed close by the place of execution. It was halted, so as to make an impression on the Muscovites.

But a cry rang out, followed by two others. Three prisoners dashed forward and, as they were not chained, threw themselves on the body of the executed prisoner who had just received the eleven thousandth stroke of the rod. They fell on their knees and, shedding copious tears, kissed with devotion Mony's bloodstained head. The Japanese soldiers, momentarily stupefied, soon realized that though one of the prisoners was a man, a colossus even, the two others were pretty women disguised as soldiers. It was in fact Cornaboeux, Culculine and Alexine, who had been captured after the Russian army's catastrophe.

At first the Japanese respected their grief, then, aroused by the two women, they began to make free with them. Cornaboeux was left on his knees beside his master's body and Culculine and Alexine, who struggled in vain, were de-bagged.

The fine white and rippling arses of these pretty Parisiennes were soon apparent to the wonderstruck gaze of the soldiers. Gently and passionlessly they set to thwacking these delightful posteriors which bobbed about like drunken moons, and when the pretty creatures were trying to get up, the fur on their yawning pussies was visible below.

The strokes swished through the air and, falling flat but not too hard, momentarily marked the firm and fleshy arses of the Parisiennes, but the marks soon faded, to regroup on whatever spot the cane had freshly landed.

When they had become suitably excited, two Japanese officers led them away to a tent and there fucked them ten or a dozen times in the manner of men ravenous after prolonged abstinence.

These Japanese officers were gentlemen from noble families. They had undertaken espionage in France and knew Paris. Culculine and Alexine had no difficulty getting them to promise that Prince Vibescu's body would be surrendered to them, since they claimed him as their cousin and passed themselves off as sisters.

Amongst the prisoners was a French journalist, a correspondent for a provincial newspaper. Before the war he had been a sculptor, not without talent, and his name was Genmolay. Culculine sought him out to invite him to sculpt a monument worthy of the memory of Prince Vibescu.

Flogging was Genmolay's main passion. All he requested of Culculine was to flog her. She accepted, and arrived at the appointed time with Alexine and Cornaboeux. The two women and the two men stripped naked. Alexine and Culculine disposed themselves on a bed, heads down and arses aloft, and the two brawny Frenchmen, armed with canes, started beating them so that most of the blows would fall on their arsecracks or cunts which, owing to the posture, jutted out admirably. They were laying about them, working themselves up. The two women were suffering martyrdom, but the notion that their pains would procure a proper sepulchre for Mony sustained them to the end of this singular ordeal.

Then Genmolay and Cornaboeux sat down and had their big sap-filled pricks sucked off, while with their canes they went on smiting the trembling buttocks of the two pretty girls.

The next day Genmolay set to work. He had soon completed an astonishing monument. The equestrian statue of Prince Mony surmounted it.

On the pedestal were bas-reliefs representing the prince's brilliant feats of arms. On one side he was to be seen leaving a beseiged Port Arthur by balloon, and on the other he was portrayed as patron of the arts that he had gone to study in Paris.

The traveller who crosses the Manchurian plain between Mukden[33] and Dalny suddenly notices, not far from a battlefield still strewn with bones, a monumental tomb in white marble. The Chinese who till the surrounding fields respect it, and the Manchurian mother, in reply to her child's questions, tells it:

--- That's a giant horseman who protected Manchuria against the devils of the West and of the East.

But the traveller generally prefers to ask the level-crossing keeper of the Transmanchurian. This watchman is a slant-eyed Japanese, in the uniform of an employee of the PLM. He replies modestly:

--- It's a Nipponese drum-major who determined the victory of Mukden.

Yet if, curious to gain precise information, the traveller approach the statue, he remains long lost in thought after reading the verse carved on the pedestal:

> *Here lies Vibescu the Prince*
> *Who made a unique lover for the eleven thousand rods*
> *Passers-by! far better, be convinced*
> *To have unmade the eleven thousand maidens with your rods*

Two:
The Memoirs Of
A Young Don Juan

◆

Chapter One

It was summertime again; my mother had returned to the country and an estate which we had only recently acquired.

My father had various business that kept him in town. He regretted buying this estate because of my mother's entreaties. 'You are the one who wanted this country house,' he would say. 'Go there if you like, but don't make me go. Besides, my dear Anna, you can be sure I shall resell it as soon as the opportunity arises.'

'But dear,' my mother would answer, 'you can't imagine how much good the country air will do the children...'

'Yes, yes, all very well,' was my father's usual retort as he consulted his notebook and reached for his hat, 'I gave in to this whim of yours but I was wrong.'

So my mother left for her country place, as she put it, determined to waste no time in enjoying to the full what might prove all too brief a luxury.

She was accompanied by a younger, still unmarried sister, a chambermaid, and myself, her only son, along with one of my sisters, a year my elder.

We arrived in fine fettle at the country house, which was known locally as The Château.

The Château, an old mansion which had once belonged to wealthy farmers, dated back to the seventeenth century. Its interior was spacious but the rooms were arranged in such an extraordinary manner that the house was actually rather inconvenient to live in, since the architecture had been haphazard.

Thus the rooms were not disposed as in ordinary houses but were separated by a mass of dark passages, winding corridors, spiral staircases. In short, the house was a veritable labyrinth, and it took several days to find one's bearings before becoming familiar with the exact layout of the rooms.

The outhouses, where the farm and its cowsheds and stables were located, were separated from the Château by a courtyard. Adjoining these buildings was a chapel which could be entered via the courtyard as well as from the main house or through the outbuildings.

This chapel was in a good state of repair. A monk had formerly officiated there, living in the Château and administering to the spiritual needs of the scattered local community which formed our modest hamlet. Since the last chaplain's death, however, the office had remained vacant, and only on Sundays and Feast Days, with occasional weekday visits to hear confessions, did a Capuchin from the nearby monastery come to our chapel to conduct those services indispensable for the worthy peasants' salvation.

When this monk came he invariably stayed for dinner and a room near the chapel was prepared for him, should he wish to spend the night there. My mother, my aunt and Kate, the maid, were busy getting the room ready, assisted by the estate manager, a farmhand and another female servant.

Since the harvest was already almost gathered in my sister and I were allowed to go for walks wherever we pleased. We scoured every nook and cranny of the Château, from cellar to attic. We would play hide and seek around the columns, or else one of us, taking refuge under a staircase, would lie in ambush waiting for the other to pass, then leap out with a bloodcurdling shriek.

The wooden staircase leading to the attic was very steep. One day I descended before Berthe did, and hid in the darkness between two chimney pipes. The staircase, by contrast, was well enough lit from the skylight above. When she appeared, coming down cautiously, I jumped out, barking loudly just like a ferocious hound. Berthe had not suspected I was there and she was so scared that she missed the next step and fell headfirst down the staircase, her legs finishing up hoisted aloft on the bottom steps.

Her dress had of course billowed back to cover her face, leaving her legs exposed. When I approached her, laughing, I observed that her blouse too had ridden up past her navel.

Berthe was not wearing any knickers because, as she later informed me, hers were dirty and no-one had had time to unpack the linen. Thus it was that for the first time I saw my sister in an immodest state.

To tell the truth I had already seen her completely naked, since we had often been bathed together during the past few years. But I had seen only the back of her, or caught a side view of her at most, because both my mother and my aunt had positioned us back to back, our diminutive bottoms cheek to cheek in the bath while we were being washed. Both ladies scrupulously ensured that there was no peeping on my part, and when they handed us our little nightgowns we were each obliged to cover ourselves, keeping both hands carefully in front of us.

One day then it transpired that Kate, who had taken my aunt's place at bathtime, was scolded for forgetting to make Berthe cover herself with her hands. As for myself, I was not so much as touched by Kate. I was always and only bathed either by my mother or aunt. When I was in the large bathtub I would be told: 'You may remove your hands now, Roger.' And as you can imagine, it was always one of them who soaped and scrubbed me. My mother, whose principle it was that children should be treated like children as long as possible, had kept this system in operation.

At that time I was thirteen and my sister Berthe fourteen. I knew nothing about love nor even about the difference between the sexes. But when I found myself naked in front of women, when I felt their soft feminine hands wandering here and there over my body, I experienced a strange agitation.

121

I remember very clearly that whenever my aunt Marguerite washed and dried my sexual parts I became conscious of a curious, vague yet extremely agreeable sensation. I noticed that my little willie would suddenly turn stiff as iron and, instead of drooping as before, would rear its head. Instinctively I used to draw closer to my aunt and thrust my belly forward as far as I could.

One day when this occurred, my aunt Marguerite promptly blushed and that flush made her delicate features all the more attractive. She had observed that my little member was erect and, pretending to take no notice, beckoned to my mother who was engaged in bathing her feet with us. Kate was meanwhile busy washing Berthe, but she also immediately became interested. I had noticed, as a matter of fact, that she far preferred taking charge of me than of my sister, and that she missed no opportunity of helping out my mother or my aunt whenever they attended to me. Now she too wanted to see what was going on.

She turned and gazed at me quite unashamedly while my aunt and my mother exchanged meaningful looks. My mother was in her petticoat and had hitched it up past her knees so she could cut her toenails more easily. This gave me a look at her pretty, plump feet, her fine muscular calves and her round white knees. The sight of my mother's legs had affected my virility as much as my aunt's fondling had done. My mother probably realised this immediately, for she blushed and let down her petticoat. The ladies smiled and Kate began laughing until stopped by disapproving glances from my mother and aunt. But she tried to excuse her behaviour by saying: 'Berthe laughs too, when I reach that place with the warm sponge.' My mother, though, ordered her to hold her tongue.

At that very moment the bathroom door opened and Elizabeth, my eldest sister, entered. She was fifteen and went to high school. Although my aunt swiftly flung a shirt over my bare body, Elizabeth had had time to see me and that bothered me considerably. For though I was not in the least embarrassed in front of Berthe, I did not want to be seen stark naked by Elizabeth, who had not had baths with us now for a good four years and in fact bathed with the ladies or with Kate.

I felt distinctly annoyed that all the females of the household had the right to come into the bathroom while I was in there, whereas I was denied a similar right. And I found it absolutely unfair to be barred admittance even when my sister Elizabeth was being bathed on her own, since I could see no reason why she should be treated differently from us, despite her ladylike airs and graces.

Berthe herself was incensed by Elizabeth's unwarranted pretensions. Elizabeth had one day refused to undress in front of her younger sister, yet did not hesitate to do so whenever my aunt and my mother were closeted with her in the bathroom.

We could not understand such behaviour, which stemmed from the fact that Elizabeth had reached puberty. Her hips were rounded, her nipples had began to swell and, as I later learned, the first pubic hair had appeared upon her mound.

That particular day Berthe had simply heard my mother say to my aunt as they were leaving the bathroom: 'With Elizabeth, it came on rather early.'

'Yes, mine was a year later.'

'Two years later in my case.'

'She'll have to have a bedroom to herself now.'

'She can share mine,' my aunt replied. Berthe had related all this to me and naturally made as little sense of it as I did.

But on this particular occasion, the moment my sister Elizabeth came in and saw me starkers with my pricklet fiercely to the fore like some enraged bantam cockerel, I noticed she could not help staring at that very spot, unable to conceal her reaction of utter astonishment. Yet she did not avert her gaze. Quite the opposite.

When my mother abruptly asked her if she too wanted to have a bath, she blushed furiously and stammered out: 'Yes, mama!'

'Roger and Berthe have finished now,' my mother said. 'You can get undressed.'

Elizabeth obeyed without demur and stripped down to her shift. I just had time to note that she was better developed than Berthe, but that was all, before I was hustled out of the bathroom. After that I was no longer bathed with Berthe. Either Aunt Marguerite or my mother would still be present because ever since my mother had read something about a child drowning in its bath she had become excessively anxious with regard to letting me bathe on my own. But the ladies, though continuing to wash the rest of my body, thereafter refrained from touching my willie or its little bollocks. There were, nevertheless, occasions when I would get an erection in front of my mother or Aunt Marguerite. The ladies did not fail to take notice, although my mother used to turn away when lifting me out and helping me on with my nightshirt, while Aunt Marguerite would stare down at the floor.

My aunt Marguerite was twenty-six years old, ten years my mother's junior, but since she had never had any great emotional upsets, she did not look her age and seemed almost like a young girl. My nudity appeared to make quite an impression on her, for each time she bathed me she adopted a softly fluty tone when speaking to me.

Once when she had thoroughly soaped and rinsed me her hand brushed my little cock. She smartly removed the hand as if it had touched a snake. I noticed this and remarked to her, somewhat vexed: 'Dear darling auntie, why don't you wash your Roger all over any more?'

She blushed deeply, replying rather uncertainly: 'But I did wash you all over!'

'Come on, auntie, wash my willie too.'

'What a naughty rascal! You can quite well wash it yourself.'

'No auntie, please, you do it. I can't do it half as well as you.'

'Oh the little rogue!' smiled my aunt, and picking up the sponge again she carefully washed my cock and balls.

'Come on, auntie darling,' I said, 'let me give you a big kiss for being so nice and kind.' And I kissed her lovely mouth, which was cherry-red and half open over sparkling and perfectly shaped teeth.

'Now dry me too,' I begged her as soon as I was out of the bath. So my aunt did dry me, lingering perhaps rather longer than strictly necessary over the sensitive area. This excited me to such a pitch that I held tight to the rim of the tub in order to thrust out my belly even further and I wriggled so agitatedly that my aunt told me gently:

'That's enough, Roger, you're not a little boy any more. From now on you'll have your bath alone.'

'Oh no, auntie, no please, not alone! You *must* bathe me. When you do it, it's so much nicer for me than when it's mother.'

'Get dressed, Roger!'

'Auntie, be nice and have a bath with me too, sometime!'

'Roger, get dressed,' she again said, moving over to the window.

'No,' I said, 'I want to see you have a bath too.'

'Roger!'

'Auntie if you won't have a bath too I'll tell Papa that you've taken my willie in your mouth again.'

My aunt blushed furiously. In fact she really had done so once, but only for a moment. It had happened one day when I didn't want my bath. The water had been too cold and I ran back into my room. My aunt had followed me in there, and as we were alone she had cuddled me a bit and ended up taking my little cock in her mouth, squeezing it between her lips for a second or two. I had enjoyed the feeling so much that I relented and became quite docile.

Anyhow, on a similar occasion my mother had done the same thing, and I know of many other instances of this practice. It happens often when women bathe little boys. For women the effect is similar to that upon us when, as men, we see or touch a young girl's little cleft, but women know better than men how to vary their pleasures.

During my earliest years I had an elderly nanny who tickled my willie and balls when I couldn't get to sleep, and sometimes she would even gently suck my cock. I seem to recollect that one day she actually placed me on her bare stomach and kept me there for some time. But all that was so long ago that my recollections are only vague ones.

As soon as my aunt had regained her composure she said to me angrily: 'That was only a joke, Roger, and you were only a little boy then. But I see now it's impossible to joke with you any more, you've grown into a man.' And she glanced again at my stiffened prick. 'What's more, you're a naughty little imp and I don't love you any more.' As she said this she gave my erection a light slap. Then she made as if to leave, but I held her back, saying:

'Forgive me, my dear auntie, I won't say a thing to anybody, even if you do get into the bathtub.'

'I can do that much, I suppose,' she smiled. She pulled her red slippers off her bare feet, hoisted her dressing gown above her knees and climbed into the bath. The water came up to the tops of her calves.

'Now I've done what you wanted, Roger, be a good boy and get dressed quietly or else I'll never look at you again.'

This with such conviction that I realised she meant what she said. I no longer had a hard-on. I picked up my nightshirt and put it on while Aunt Marguerite bathed her feet. But then, to avoid any further requests on my part, she declared she was feeling unwell and did not want a bath.

When I was decent she emerged from the bath to dry herself. The towel was wet after I'd used it. I knelt down and dried my aunt's dainty feet. She let me do so without quibbling. Whenever I wiped between her toes she laughed and when I touched and tickled the soles of her feet her good humour returned and she cheerfully agreed to let me dry her calves.

When, however, I reached her knees, she made it clear to me

I was not to go any higher. I obeyed, although for a long time I'd had a burning desire to discover what it was that women carried beneath their skirts, something so precious they were obliged to keep it carefully concealed.

My aunt and I were friends again, but since then I had had to take my baths alone. My mother doubtless learned everything from my aunt but she never did let on to me.

Now it is time to proceed from these observations, which were necessary in order to shed light on what follows. The moment has come to retrace our steps and retrieve the thread of our narrative.

Chapter Two

My sister, then, had tumbled to the foot of the stairs. She lay there with her skirt disarranged, making no effort to get up again, even when she saw me right next to her.

If not struck by lightning, she had certainly been shaken by fear and the shock of her fall. But I thought she was trying to scare me, so my curiosity outweighed any sympathy.

I could not help staring in fascination at her nakedness. Where the lower part of her belly met her thighs I saw a peculiar elevation, a fleshy mound triangular in shape, and on which some sparse blonde hairs were visible. More or less where the thighs joined, the mound was divided by a large cleft an inch or two long, forming an opening with two lips either side. I glimpsed the spot where this aperture came to an end just as my sister managed to scramble back onto her feet.

She probably had no idea how much of herself had been exposed, or else she would have pulled down her clothing at once. But suddenly she parted her thighs in order to get her feet back into position under her. That was how I saw those lips, only partially glimpsed when her thighs had been closed, and which continued, I now realised, until they converged near her buttocks.

During this quick movement of hers she had half opened her crack, at that time perhaps some three or four inches long, thus enabling me to catch sight of the red flesh inside, which contrasted with the milky whiteness of the rest of her body. Only one other area between her thighs looked slightly red, but that paler shade of red was probably due to sweat or piss.

The width of a few fingers separated her cunt, whose form resembled the curved divide of an apricot, from her arse. Thence winked Berthe's bumhole which my sister had flashed at me while turning her back to get up. This hole was no bigger than the tip of my little finger and was of a darker hue. Between her cheeks the skin was somewhat reddened by the sweat the day's heat had provoked.

My curiosity had been so intense that it never occurred to me that this fall could seriously have injured my sister, but when it did finally dawn on me I rushed to her aid. The whole incident in fact lasted less than a minute. I helped Berthe to her feet. She was shaky and complained of a headache.

There was plenty of cold water in the courtyard well, but we might have been seen and doubtless taken to task, with the result that our expeditions round the Château would have been forbidden us. So I suggested going to the far end of the garden where there was a small pond we had previously spotted from the rooftop. When we reached it we found, almost hidden amid dense undergrowth, some man-made boulders between which a spring flowed into the pond.

Berthe sat down on a stone bench and using our handkerchiefs I made her some compresses. She was breathless and rather overheated. But it was well before noon, and after about half an hour she had more or less recovered although she still sported a large bump on her head. This no one would see, luckily, since her hair hid it.

During all this time I recalled and mentally listed everything I had just seen, letting my mind linger in the pleasant contemplation of these new discoveries. Yet I had no notion as to how, in the light of them, I should act with Berthe.

Finally I decided what to do. When I had seen my sister naked I'd noticed that at the base of her bush, just where her cunt ended, there was a beauty spot. I too had a similar sort of mole just below my balls.

One day my mother and my aunt had looked at it laughingly and I had not understood why; later, examining my arse in the mirror I had seen it. When I confided as much to Berthe she blushed crimson and seemed very surprised. At first she pretended not to understand, but when I'd described its position, lying down on the ground with my legs spread out to demonstrate to her just how I'd seen it, she was clearly smitten with embarrassment.

I now ensured that we were quite alone in the garden. The vegetation was high enough to hide us from prying eyes from afar, while we ourselves would soon be aware of any outsider's approach.

I unbuttoned my braces, dropped my light summer trousers and lay on my back, facing my sister.

'Gracious, Roger! What if someone were to see you!' she said, half to herself, though without averting her gaze.

'There's nobody about, Berthe,' I replied in the same hushed tones. Then I stood up in front of her, raised my shirt and said: 'Since I've seen all of you, you can see all of me.'

Berthe's curiosity was aroused and she looked at me quite without embarrassment. Her gaze began to have an effect on me: my member hardened, rose slowly, then lolloped upright self-importantly, its knob unsheathed.

'You see Berthe, I piss through the little hole at the end, but now I can't, even though I want to.'

'I've been dying to go, too, for ages,' Berthe said softly, 'but I'm ashamed to. You mustn't look at me, Roger!'

'Don't be so pathetic, Berthe. Anyway, if you hold it too long your bladder will burst and you'll die. That's what our old nurse used to say.'

Berthe got up, glanced round, then crouched down beside the bench and began pissing. I leaned over quickly so I could see everything and did see a thin but steady stream spurting from the top of her cleft and falling obliquely to the ground.

'Hey, Roger, no!' she whimpered, 'that's not nice!' She finished pissing and stood up again.

'But Berthe, no one can see us,' was my rejoinder, 'so don't be like that.' I smiled, adding: 'Look at me, I'm not shy in front of you.' I began to piss, but in irregular jerks because my member was still stiff. Berthe burst out laughing. I took advantage of her jollity by deftly lifting her skirt and blouse. Then I made her squat and forced her to piss.

She no longer resisted but spread her legs and bent forward slightly. I watched the stream splash down over the ground before slackening off. My sister seemed to be straining somewhat by the end, and her crack opened right at the top to reveal the red flesh. All this lasted a matter of seconds. The stream dwindled and only a few drops dribbled down.

Then, using both hands I grasped the lips of her cunt and drew them apart. This she seemed greatly to enjoy, for otherwise she would not have kept her skirt raised so obligingly.

The upshot was, I discovered that her cleft, comparable to a half-open mussel, contained two additional lips far smaller than the outside pair. Their colour was a beautiful deep red and they were closed. Above them was a small hole through which she had pissed. Also visible was a tiny outcrop of flesh about the size of a pea. I touched it, finding it to be extremely hard.

These gropings seemed to please my sister, since she remained motionless, other than thrusting out her belly slightly. She became very excited and lifted her blouse and skirt well above her navel. So then I moved on to her belly, my hands roving to explore everywhere. I tickled her navel and scoured it with my tongue. Then I drew back a bit for a better view.

Only then did I see the delightful down adorning Berthe's plump triangular mound.

Actually the hairs were sparse, short and downy and so fair that only by looking very closely could they be discerned at all. As for myself, my own crop was scarcely any thicker, but the hairs were darker.

I twiddled them a little and evinced a certain astonishment as to the difference in colour of our respective pubic hair. Berthe, however, replied: 'It's always the way!'

'How do you know?'

'Kate told me when we were alone in the bath once. Anyhow, I'm going to have my periods soon.'

'What's that?'

'Several days each month blood pours out of the hole. Kate had hair and periods when she was my age.'

'Does she have hair like yours?'

'Of course not!' said Berthe in a superior manner. And, letting her clothes fall back into place, she added: 'Kate has red hair down there and mine is blonde. She puts oil on her head to make her hair look darker. Anyway, she has so much hair down below that you can't see her thingy unless she opens her legs really wide.'

While Berthe had been talking my member had lost its stiffness. Berthe noticed this and said: 'Look, your thing has gone small again. Kate told me all about that one day when I asked her why she'd laughed in the bathroom. She said your member had stuck up straight, like a man's. She seemed to think it was pretty big, too. "If he were a man," she also said, "I'd let him do it to me good and proper. Watch out, Berthe, in case he tries doing it to you".'

'What's that mean: doing it?' I inquired.

'Well, when people sort of rub against each other. Kate's already done it to me and I had to do it to her too. It was far nicer with her than what you did just now. She always wets her finger. She made me stick my thumb up her because apparently that's the finger which goes in furthest. So then I moved it quickly backwards and forwards and she absolutely loved it. She did it to me and I loved it too, but the first time she made me do it to her she really scared me. She began sighing and gasping then she started yelling and shuddering all over. I thought there was

133

something the matter with her and she was ill and I'd better stop. "Don't stop, Berthe," she told me, and she was shaking all over by then and crying out "Berthe, Berthe, it's coming, oh, oh, oh!...."

'Then she fell back onto the bed as if she'd fainted. When I took my finger out of her crack it was kind of gluey. She made me wash, and promised me she'd make me come like that too when I was older and had hair down there.'

A thousand thoughts crossed my mind. I had hundreds of questions I wanted to ask, because there was still a lot I didn't understand.

Who knows what might have happened if the dinner bell had not rung. I took one last look at Berthe's treasures and showed her mine. Then we both rearranged our clothes. Finally we kissed, promising on our word of honour to keep what had transpired between us a secret. We were just about to leave when the sound of voices stopped us in our tracks.

Chapter Three

We then realised that the bell which had just rung was not for us, but to summon the servants to supper. So we were in no particular hurry to leave, now that we were dressed. No-one happening to pass by could have had any inkling of what we'd been up to.

The sound of voices which we had originally heard nearby came from beyond the garden. We soon saw that the voices were those of some servant girls who had been working in the field just behind the garden. But we could observe them at leisure now, since the servants' supper did not actually begin until a quarter of an hour after the bell.

It had rained the previous night and the freshly ploughed soil clung to the girls' bare feet. Their skirts – or rather, skirt, for in fact each girl was apparently wearing only one – seemed very short, scarcely reaching the knee. They were not especially attractive, yet they were well-built, these sun-tanned peasant girls whose ages ranged from twenty to thirty.

When they reached the water they sat down on the grassy bank by the stream and soaked their feet in it. While bathing their feet they started jabbering away as if in competition with one another.

They were right opposite us, a matter of ten paces or so, and this meant we could clearly distinguish the striking contrast between their brown calves and far whiter knees. The latter were now completely exposed, and with a few of the girls even a hint of thigh was visible.

Berthe was evidently not enjoying this spectacle in the least and she was tugging my arm with a view to our leaving. But then we heard footsteps close by and saw three farmhands approaching along a pathway very near us. At the sight of these men several of the servant girls adjusted their clothing. One of them was very particular in this respect, a girl whose coal-black hair and mischievous clear grey eyes suggested Spanish blood.

The first labourer, an oafish yokel, completely ignored the women's presence and, standing directly in front of our hiding place, unbuttoned his trousers to piss. He took out his member, which looked much like mine except that his glans was fully concealed. He unhooded it to piss. He had raised his shirt-tails so high that the hair surrounding his genitals was visible. He had also hauled his balls out of his trousers and was scratching them with his left hand while directing his member with the right.

I was just as bored by this as Berthe had been when I'd pointed out to her the peasant girls' calves, but now she was all eyes. The girls were pretending not to notice the performance. The second labourer also unbuttoned himself and likewise produced his prick, smaller than his predecessor's but brownish and with tip half-exposed. He began pissing. At that the girls burst out laughing and their shrieks grew uncontrollable when the third fellow also took up position.

By this time the first one had finished. He pulled back his foreskin all the way, shook his cock to get rid of the last few drops, and bent his knees slightly to replace the package in his trousers. In so doing he unleashed a loud, emphatic fart and emitted also an audible sigh of satisfaction. This sent the girls into stitches, their derisive laughter rising to a crescendo.

The hilarity actually increased when they noticed the third labourer's implement. This lout was standing at a slight angle, which allowed us to see both his tool and the peasant girls beyond. He pointed it up in the air so that the jet would fountain aloft, thus giving the farm wenches hysterics. Then the men went across to the women and one of the latter began playfully splashing water over the doltish farmhand. The third man commented to the brunette who, seeing men in the offing, had rearranged her clothes:

'No good hiding it, Ursula. I've already seen that precious whatsit of yours.'

'Plenty of things you haven't yet seen, Valentin, and a whole lot you'll never see,' Ursula flirtatiously replied.

'That so?' said Valentin, who was now standing right behind her. As he spoke, he seized her shoulders and shoved her backward to the ground. She tried to get her feet out of the water, but neglected to stop her skimpy skirt and blouse billowing back, so she ended up in the identical position as my sister a while earlier. Unfortunately this charming exhibition lasted only a few seconds.

It had nevertheless lasted just long enough to demonstrate that Ursula, who'd already shown she possessed a pair of splendid calves, was also the proud owner of beautiful, nay prize-winning, thighs, together with a peerless arse whose buttocks left nothing to be desired. Intercrurally, below her belly, lay a bush of black hair descending extensively enough to envelop both her pretty cunt-lips, but there she was not quite so hirsute as above, where her hairs encompassed an area my hand would scarcely have managed to cover.

'You see, Ursula,' said the considerably excited Valentin, 'now I've seen your little black mousey too!'

And he unflinchingly bore a rain of blows and insults from the young woman, who was by now in a real rage.

The second farmhand wanted to follow suit with another of the girls, trying it on as Valentin had done with Ursula. This other peasant girl was attractive enough, and her neck and arms were so freckled that it was virtually impossible to distinguish her natural skin colour. Her legs also had freckles on them, but fewer and larger ones. She looked intelligent, a brown-eyed, curly-haired redhead. She wasn't what you'd call pretty, but appetising enough to give a man ideas. And the hired hand Michel seemed to have acquired a few: 'Hélène,' he said, 'you ought to have a red bush. If it's black, you must have pinched it from somewhere!'

'Dirty lout!' the charming girl retorted.

He grabbed her, taking a leaf out of Valentin's book.

But she had had time to rise to her feet, and instead of a flash of her pretty quim, Michel received such a barrage of blows full in the face that he must have seen a few dozen stars at the very least. Two other girls joined in, pummelling him relentlessly. Shouting protests, he finally managed to escape, pursued by mocking female laughter, and off he ran after his companions.

The farmgirls had finished washing their feet and had left. Only Ursula and Hélène remained and they too were getting ready to depart. They were whispering together. Ursula burst out laughing and pulled a face, wrinkling her forehead. Hélène was standing over her, looking at her and nodding assent.

The former seemed to be thinking about what Hélène had told her. Hélène glanced around to ensure that everyone had gone, then quickly raised her skirt in front, holding it up and out with her left hand. Meanwhile her right went between her thighs, to the spot which boasted a thicket of russet hair. From the movement of the hair, so much thicker than Ursula's, one could see she was squeezing between her fingers the lips of her cunt, amply concealed by the thickness of its fleece.

Ursula calmly watched her. Suddenly a stream shot from the hairy bush, but instead of falling straight to the ground it described something of an arc in the air. Berthe was as amazed as I myself, for neither of us knew a woman could piss like that.

It lasted just as long as with Valentin. Ursula was utterly astonished and seemed to want to try it herself, but she gave up the idea when the second and last bell for supper rang and the two girls dashed off hurriedly.

Chapter Four

When Berthe and I returned to the Château we found the table laid. But my mother and my aunt had not yet quite finished arranging the room. While my sister was helping them I read the newspaper my father used to send on to us. There was a report concerning a Monsieur X... who had violated a Mademoiselle A... and I duly looked up the word *violate* in the dictionary and found: 'to deflower'. I was none the wiser than before, although I had yet more food for thought.

At last everyone sat down to eat, and Berthe and I, contrary to our usual behaviour, exchanged not a word. This astonished my mother and my aunt, who concluded 'They must have been fighting again.' To us it seemed preferable to conceal our newfound intimacy under the feigned mantle of spite.

My mother explained how they had organised the rooms, father and herself in one, and another for my aunt. The rooms were on the first floor, along with those reserved for Kate and for Berthe.

Mine was on the ground floor, behind a flight of stairs leading to the library. I went up to the library later, and found it contained numerous old books along with a few more recent works.

The room prepared for the friar was next to the library. A corridor separated this one from the chapel. In the chapel, by the altar, were two large stalls where the former proprietors came and sat for Mass. Behind one of these stalls was the lord of the manor's confessional, whereas the other box, for the servants' use, was situated at the far end of the chapel.

I must have noted all this at some point after the meal, since

Berthe had had to go and help the ladies. There'd scarcely been time to give her a kiss, under the pretext of seeing if I too could render any assistance.

Several days passed without anything much happening. Berthe was kept constantly busy by the womenfolk, who had not yet finished getting the house in order.

Since the weather was awful I spent most of my time in the library, where I'd been pleasantly surprised to discover an atlas of anatomy in which I found detailed illustrations and a description of the male and female reproductive organs. The book also included a full explanation of pregnancy in all its various stages, and none of this had I previously known about. The latter information particularly interested me since the estate manager's wife was then pregnant, and her enormous belly had greatly aroused my curiosity. I had overheard her discussing her condition with her husband. Their quarters were on the ground floor next to mine, on the garden side.

Needless to say, the events of that memorable day when I had seen my sister naked, followed by the incident of the male and female workers exposing themselves, remained uppermost in my mind. I dwelt upon them incessantly and had what seemed like an endless hard-on. I frequently inspected and played with my member. The pleasure I derived when fingering it incited me to continue.

I used to amuse myself in bed by lying face down and rubbing my loins against the sheet. My sensations became daily more heightened. A week passed in this way.

One day, seated in the old leather chair in the library, and with the atlas spread open across my lap at the page describing the female genitalia, I had such an erection that I unbuttoned my flies and took out my prick. Through constant rubbing, my member now uncovered easily. I was, too, sixteen by this time, and considered myself a man. My pubic hair had sprouted more thickly and now resembled a fine bushy moustache. That particular day

I felt so profound and unaccustomed a voluptuousness as I frigged and frotted that breathing became an effort. I tightened my grasp upon my member, loosened it, and rubbed to and fro along the shaft. I pulled back the foreskin fully, tickled my bollocks and arsehole, then examined my exposed glans, which had taken on a deep red tone and shone like lacquer. The pleasure I felt was quite indescribable. I wound up discovering the rules of the fine art of masturbation, and manipulated my dick regularly and rhythmically to such effect that something happened of which I had hitherto been ignorant.

A feeling of unspeakable pleasure made me stretch my legs out in front of me and push against the table-legs, while my body slid down and pressed against the back of the armchair. I felt my face flush. Breathing grew difficult. I found I had to close my eyes and open my mouth. In the space of a moment or two a thousand thoughts raced through my head.

My aunt, in front of whom I had stood naked, my sister whose pretty little pussy I'd viewed, the two farmgirls and their powerful thighs – all these images whirled through my mind. My hand tugged faster and faster at my prick and an electric shock coursed through my body.

My aunt! Berthe! Ursula! Hélène!... I felt my member swell, and from the dark red glans spurted forth a whitish substance, a thick jet to start with, followed by a series of lesser squirts. I had just discharged for the first time.

My engine rapidly turned limp: I now looked with interest and curiosity at the sperm which had spilled into my right palm. It looked and smelled like the white of an egg and was thick as glue. I licked it and found it tasted like raw egg. I shook off the last few drops clinging to the tip of my now completely subdued member, which I wiped on my shirt.

I knew from previous reading that I had just indulged in onanism. I'd looked up the word in the dictionary and found a lengthy article on the subject, going into such detail that anyone hitherto unaware of the practice would indubitably have been enlightened. This piece of reading excited me afresh.

The fatigue resulting from my first ejaculation had disappeared. An overwhelming hunger proved to be the only outcome of this act. At table my aunt and my mother remarked upon my appetite, but attributed it to growing pains. I soon came to realise that onanism is like drink: the more you have, the more you want...

My prick was continually hard and my thoughts increasingly sensual, but the pleasures of Onan could not satisfy me for ever. I would think about women and it seemed a shame to waste my sperm wanking.

My tool turned darker, my pubic hair grew into a handsome goatee, my voice deepened, and some paltry microscopic hairs burgeoned on my upper lip. I realised that I lacked only one experience of manhood: *coitus* – the term the books used for that activity as yet unknown to me.

All the women of the household noticed the changes that had taken place in me, and I was no longer treated as a child.

Chapter Five

The Château's patron Saint's Day was at hand, the occasion for a major celebration preceded by all members of the household making their confessions. My mother and my aunt had both decided to go to confession and the others would shortly follow their example. I had managed to pretend I was unwell and had kept to my room since the previous evening, so that my supposed indisposition would arouse no suspicion.

The Capuchin had arrived and dined with us. Coffee had been served in the garden, and there I remained on my own after Kate had finished clearing the table. As time was weighing heavy on my hands I went into the library, where I chanced upon a secret entrance which I'd never noticed before. This door gave on to a narrow and dark concealed staircase illuminated only by a tiny bull's eye window set into the far end of the upstairs corridor.

The stairs led to the chapel, and from behind the bolted door rusty from many years of disuse, the Capuchin's voice could be heard. He was telling my mother he would hear her confession there the following day. Through the wooden partition which backed the confessional every word was clearly audible. So it seemed to me that here would be the ideal vantage point from which to eavesdrop. It also occurred to me that this flight of stairs must have been installed centuries ago by some jealous seigneur who wanted to overhear his wife's confessions.

The next morning after coffee, the estate manager's wife came in to make my bed and tidy up the room. I have mentioned her pregnancy earlier, but now I had time for a leisurely inspection of the enormous bulk of her belly, and the exceptional size of her breasts which were bouncing about beneath her light blouse. She was a pleasant woman with quite an attractive face. Before she married the estate manager who'd put her in the family way, she had been one of the Château's maids.

I had already seen women's breasts in pictures and on statues, but never in the flesh.

The estate manager's wife was pressed for time. She had fastened only one of her blouse buttons. When she bent over to make my bed this button too came undone and I saw her entire bosom, for her blouse was very lowcut. I jumped up: 'Madame, you'll catch cold like that!' And pretending to help her rebutton the blouse, I undid the neck ribbon which kept it up.

Simultaneously the two nipples seemed to leap from their hiding place and I realised just how big and firm they were. Each breast's bud stood out in relief: these were red and surrounded by very large and brownish areoles. Her knockers were as firm as a pair of buttocks, and as my hands fondled them I might almost have mistaken them for a pretty girl's backside.

The woman was so nonplussed that before she recovered her wits I had ample time to kiss her tits. She smelled of sweat, but the scent was so nice that I grew excited. It was that *odor di femina* which, as I later learned, emanates from a woman's body and, according to the individual, provokes either desire or disgust.

'Ah! Ooh! What's come over you... No... that's not right!... I'm a married woman... not for anything in the world...'

These were her words as I was steering her towards the bed. I had opened my dressing gown and raised my nightshirt, to show her my member in its frantically excited state.

'Let me go, I'm pregnant! Oh Lord God, if anyone should see us!'

She was still putting up a resistance, albeit less vigorously. As a matter of fact, her gaze had not left my sexual parts. She was supporting herself against the bed onto which I was trying to push her.

'You're hurting me!'

'My dear lady, no one can see or hear you.'

Now she was sitting on the bed. I continued to push. She weakened, lay back and shut her eyes. My state of excitation was beyond all bounds. I hauled up her petticoats, skirt and blouse and saw a fine pair of thighs which fired my enthusiasm even more than the peasant girls' had done. Between the closed thighs I caught sight of a small thatch of chestnut-coloured hairs effectively concealing the crack. I fell upon my knees, seized her thighs, felt them all over, caressed them, pressed my cheeks against them and kissed them. My lips progressed from her thighs up to the mound of Venus, where the smell of urine excited me still further. I lifted her skirt even higher and looked in astonishment at the huge bulk of her stomach, whose navel protruded instead of dimpling like my sister's.

I licked this belly button. She lay motionless, her breasts now flopping sideways. I picked up one of her legs and laid it along the bed. Her cunt came into view. I was scared at first, when I saw the two big thick puffy lips coloured a reddish brown. Her pregnancy gave me full opportunity to revel in the sight. Her lips were spread, and when I darted a glance inside I discovered a veritable butcher's stall of moist red meat.

Near the top of the labia majora could be seen the piss-hole, crowned by a tiny nub of flesh which I knew from my study of the anatomical atlas to be the clitoris. The upper part of her slit was lost in the hair covering her excessively plump mound of Venus. The lips themselves were almost hairless and the skin between the thighs was damp and red with sweat.

All in all, not a very appetising spectacle, but I appreciated it nonetheless because the woman was very clean. I could not help putting my tongue into her crevice and I rapidly licked and guzzled at the clitoris which hardened under my frenzied tonguing.

I soon tired of this lingual sport, and the crack was sopping wet so I exchanged tongue for finger. Then I seized hold of her breasts, taking her nipples into my mouth and sucking each in turn. My index finger remained on the clitoris, which grew harder and larger until it seemed almost on a par with my little finger and as thick as a pencil. At that point the woman came to her senses and began whimpering, though without abandoning the position into which I had forced her. I felt slightly sorry for her but was too worked up to really care. I murmured to her cajolingly in order to comfort her and ended up promising to stand as godfather to the child she was expecting.

I went over to a drawer and handed her some money from it. She had by then rearranged her disordered clothing. So I lifted my own nightshirt, feeling somewhat ashamed to find myself naked again in front of a woman, especially one who was married and pregnant.

I took the moist hand of the estate manager's wife and placed it upon my member. The touch of it was truly exquisite. First she squeezed gently, then more firmly. I had grasped her tits which were fascinating me. I kissed her on the mouth and she eagerly gave me her lips. My whole being was attuned to pleasure. I positioned myself between her thighs but she exclaimed: 'Not on top of me, that hurts. I can't do it the front way any more.'

She got off the bed, turned round and bent over with her face on the bed. She said nothing else, but my instinct gave me the answer to the riddle. I remembered once seeing two dogs in action. I immediately followed Médor's example and lifted her skirts. Diane, that was her name.

Her arse was displayed to view, but such a butt as I'd never even dreamed of. Berthe's bottom was pert enough and in some ways more appealing but it was really nothing compared to this. My two cheeks put together wouldn't have added up to even half of one of these miraculous and far from flabby buttocks. Like all beautiful breasts and thighs, her bum was a dazzling white. In the slit there were blonde hairs, and the crack itself formed a great divide between the two superb cheeks of this amazing arse.

Below the colossal buttocks, between the thighs, lay the fat juicy cunt into which my jovial finger foraged. I placed my chest against the woman's bare backside and with my arms tried encircling her elusive belly pendulous as some majestic globe. Then I kissed her cheeks and rubbed my member between them. But my curiosity was still not satisfied. I parted her cheeks and inspected her arsehole. Like her navel, it was in relief, and brown too, but very clean.

I made as if to insert my finger, but she gave such a start that I was afraid I had hurt her and so did not press the point. I placed my burning prick into her cunt, like a knife slicing into a slab of butter. Then I went at it like a demon, slapping my belly against her rubbery behind.

It drove me absolutely out of my mind. I was no longer conscious of what I was doing, and that was how I reached the voluptuous climax and for the first time ejaculated my sperm into a woman's cunt.

After the discharge I wanted to linger awhile in that agreeable position, but the estate manager's wife turned round and chastely covered up again. While she was rebuttoning her camisole I heard an infinitesimal splashing, the sound of my sperm as it trickled from her cunt to drip down onto the floor. She smeared it underfoot and rubbed between her thighs with her skirt to dry herself off.

When she saw me standing in front of her, my wet reddened prick partly erect, she smiled, took out her handkerchief and meticulously cleaned up the member which had enjoyed her.

'Get dressed now, Monsieur Roger,' she said. 'I have to go now. And for the love of God,' she added, blushing, 'don't let anyone find out what happened just now, or I'll never forgive you.'

I held her close, we exchanged kisses, and she departed, leaving me beset by such a spate of new sensations that I almost forgot about the confessions.

Chapter Six

Wearing an ancient pair of slippers, I entered the narrow corridor as quietly as possible. I reached the wooden partition and soon found the best area from which to eavesdrop. The Capuchin had organised things so that the person confessing would be alone in the oratory, while those waiting their turn remained in the chapel.

Thus there was no need for anyone to speak in hushed tones, and the conversation was quite distinct. I inferred from the voice that a peasant was now in the confessional. The confession must have been in progress for some time, since the Capuchin was talking as follows:

The Confessor – So you're saying you always play with your member in the lavatory. Why do you? How long do you play with it, and does this happen often?

The Peasant – Generally twice a week, but sometimes every day, until I come. I can't help it, it makes me feel so good.

The Confessor – And haven't you ever done it with women?

The Peasant – Only once, with an old woman.

The Confessor – Tell me about that, and don't keep anything back.

The Peasant – I was up in the hayloft once, with old Rosalie. I began to get a hard-on, and I said: 'Rosalie, is it a long time since you had a man?' And she said 'Oh you dirty dog, well I never! It must be forty years ago, if it's a day. And I can't say I want another. I'm sixty, you know.' I answered: 'Come on, Rosalie, I wouldn't half mind seeing a woman starkers, just once. Get them off, go on.' She said: 'No, I wouldn't dare, the devil might appear.' So I said: 'The last time you did it he didn't show up.' Then I

149

pulled up the ladder so no-one could climb up. And pulled out my cock and showed it to her. She looked at it and said: 'Why, it's even bigger than that bastard Jean's was.' So I said to her: 'Now Rosalie, you've got to show me your cunt.' She didn't want to show me a thing, but I jerked her skirts up over her head and had a good look...

The Confessor – Well then, what happened in the end?

The Peasant – She had a big gash under her belly. It was purple, like an overripe damson, and above it was a bush of grey hairs.

The Confessor – That's not what I asked you. What was it you did?

The Peasant – I stuffed my sausage into her slit, right up to the balls, which couldn't fit in. As soon as I was inside, Rosalie began moving her belly to and fro, shouting: 'Hold me under my bottom, pig! Get your hands there and move like I'm doing'. Then we both started moving about together, so I started getting really hot and Rosalie wiggled around so much that, saving your presence, she came five or six times. Then I came once, saving your presence. Then Rosalie began yelling: 'Squeeze me tighter, you swine, I'm coming, I'm coming!' and then I did too, all over again. But they sacked her because one of the stable girls had overheard us and spilled the beans. And that's why I don't want to go chasing after the young sluts.

The Confessor – A fine bunch of mortal sins! What else have you on your conscience?

The Peasant – I always used to think about Rosalie. One day in the cowshed while the farmgirls were away having something to eat, I see one of the cows is in heat. I think to myself, *she's got a cunt just like Rosalie's*. I get my prick out and try shoving it into the cow. But she didn't stay put like Rosalie did. I lifted her tail, though, and kept it in. So I managed to screw her and enjoyed it even more than with Rosalie. But she shat on me, saving your presence, and my balls and trousers were covered in it. Which is why I never wanted to screw her again.

The Confessor – Yes, but how could you do such things?

The Peasant – Our shepherd does the same with the goats and our hired girl Lucie lay down in the stable one day with the big gander between her thighs, because it's really good for the belly, so she said to the girl with her, who had a go too.

The rest of the confession was of no interest. I left my hideyhole and dashed into the chapel to have a look at the penitent's face. I was amazed to find it was the doltish fellow who had so idiotically become the butt of the peasant girls by the pond. He was the last male to confess.

My mother rose to make her confession. Kneeling beside her were my aunt and the saucy Kate. Behind them in the pews were all the maids. I was surprised not to see my sister Berthe there. The estate manager's wife had been excused confession because of her advanced state of pregnancy.

My mother's confession was very innocent, but interesting all the same: 'I've got something else to ask you, Father,' she said, after enumerating her daily sins. 'For some time now my husband has been making certain demands. On our wedding night he made me strip naked, and on several occasions since he has made me do so too. But now he always wants to see me naked, and he showed me an old book written by a priest, which says, among other things: "Married couples must perform the carnal act completely naked, so that the man's seed may mix more intimately with the female fluid." The older I get, though, the more qualms I have about this matter.'

The Confessor – This book was written in the Middle Ages. In those days it was not the general rule to wear nightshirts. Only persons of high station wore them. Common folk slept shirtless in the conjugal bed, and even nowadays there are country areas where this custom persists. Our peasant women, for instance, almost all sleep thus, mainly because of bedbugs. The Church does not look upon this practice with an approving eye, but nor does it expressly forbid it.

My Mother – You've reassured me on this point. But my husband also insists I adopt certain positions I'm ashamed of. Recently I had to get down naked on all fours while he watched me from behind. Each time I have to parade round the room in the nude he gives me a swagger-stick and shouts commands – 'Forward march!, Halt!, By the right, Quick march!' – and so on, just like a military drill.

The Confessor – This shouldn't really be happening, but if you submit to it only out of duty, you commit no sin.

My Mother – Ah, there is one more thing still on my mind, but I'm ashamed to mention it.

The Confessor – There is no sin too great to be absolved, my daughter. Unburden your conscience.

My Mother – My husband is forever wanting to take me from the rear and he behaves in such a way that I nearly faint with shame. Lately I've felt him putting his finger covered with ointment into my... my... anus. I try to stand upright again, he reassures me, but I feel him going on to insert his member. It hurt me at first, but after a while, why I don't know, it felt pleasant, and when he's finished I have the same sensation as if he'd gone in the natural way. (The rest was whispered too quietly for me to distinguish.)

The Confessor – That is a sin. Send your husband to me for confession.

The remainder of her confession was boring. Soon afterwards my aunt took her place, and I heard the pleasant sound of her voice. From what I could gather she was apologising for often missing confession. But I was thunderstruck on hearing her add, in low, hesitant tones, that she, who had never before felt any carnal desires, had been moved to passionate lust upon seeing her young nephew in the bath, and that she had libidinously touched his body but had been able in the nick of time to restrain these wicked desires. Except once when her nephew was sleeping and the bedcover had slipped down, leaving his virile organs exposed. She had stood looking at him for a long time and had even taken his member in her mouth. All this emerged with difficulty, as the words seemed to stick in her throat. I experienced an extraordinary upsurge of emotion.

The Confessor – Have you never sinned with men, or haven't you ever even polluted yourself when alone?

My Aunt – I'm still a virgin, at least where men are concerned. I've often looked at myself in the mirror, and I've touched myself and felt my private parts with my hand. Once... (She hesitated.)

The Confessor – Courage, my child! Hide nothing from your confessor.

My Aunt – Once my sister said to me: 'Our maid uses up an awful lot of candles. She's obviously reading novels in bed, and one of these nights she'll end up setting the house on fire. You sleep near her, so you be careful!' That very evening, when I saw a light in the maid's room, here's what I did. I'd left the door open and tiptoed noiselessly into Kate's room. She was sitting on the floor with her back half turned to me, and leaning towards her bed. In front of her was a chair with a mirror on it, and to the left and right of the mirror two candles were burning. Kate was in a nightgown and I distinctly observed in the mirror that she was holding something long and white and was manipulating this with both hands, back and forth between her thighs, which were wide apart. She was sighing deeply and trembling all over. Suddenly I heard her cry: 'Oh, oh, aah! it feels so good!' She bowed her head, shut her eyes and seemed dead to the world. Then I moved and she sprang to her feet. I saw she was holding an almost concealed candle. Whereupon she explained to me she was doing it in memory of her lover who had been conscripted into the army. I expressed amazement that anybody could do such a thing, but she begged me not to tell anyone. I left, but the spectacle had left such a mark on me that afterwards, Father, I couldn't help trying the same thing, and alas! I've often repeated it since. Yes, I've sunk lower still, Father. I've frequently taken off my nightdress and, following Kate's example, and in various different positions, have given myself up to sinful pleasures.

The confessor recommended she get married, and gave her absolution.

The reader can easily guess, in the light of my sister's confidences and my aunt's confession, what Kate's own confession consisted of. I learned, too, that she yearned more and more to have a man, and that her friendship with Berthe was becoming closer by the day. They often slept together in the nude and frequently compared their arses in the mirror, after mutual examination of the rest of their bodies.

The maids' confessions were all straightforward. They'd let the hired men fuck them, but there'd been no fancy stuff, and they'd never let a man enter their shared bedroom where they all slept together, naked. But during the military exercises all their precautions had proved fruitless. A regiment had been billeted throughout the neighbourhood and there had been soldiers everywhere. Thus all the girls, including even one who was getting on in years, had allowed themselves to be fucked, even buggered, which to them seemed like a mortal sin. When the Capuchin questioned them whether they had masturbated alone or with a girlfriend, one replied: 'Who'd want to stick her hand up a smelly cunt?' But they saw nothing wrong in watching each other shit or piss, nor in having used chickens, pigeons or geese to make themselves come.

One of them had once let a dog lick her cunt. When asked if she had let it screw her she answered: 'I'd have been only too glad to, but he wasn't big enough.'

I took every possible precaution to avoid being seen as I returned to my room.

154

Chapter Seven

Shortly after I had returned to my room, my mother and my aunt came in to inform me of my father's impending visit. They told me, too, that Berthe was unwell and had been confined to bed. My mother added that the illness was nothing serious and Berthe would soon be recovered, but that meanwhile it would be best if I did not go in to see her.

This all aroused my curiosity and it took me next to no time to decide what I would do. I knew that my mother and my aunt were to accompany the Capuchin into the village, making an afternoon call on an impoverished woman who was sick, and that Kate was due to go with them, taking along a basket of clothes for her.

While the ladies were talking, I scrutinised them closely, seeing them in completely new light as a result of their confessions. The dark, rather austere clothes they were wearing accentuated their most distinctive features, my mother's blooming complexion and my aunt's unusually slim waist. They were equally desirable: one, whose virginity was as yet undespoiled by masculine contact, but holding out promise of unimaginable voluptuousness; the other, the experienced and mature married woman who had freely acceded to all the lustful games an inventive and sensual husband might devise.

As they entered my room I was washing, so I explained I had been trying to get up, for actually my feigned illness was beginning to bore me considerably. My aunt, who had not seen my room or the library until now, wandered off into the latter. My

155

mother went back to the kitchen to supervise the preparation of the next meal.

Being left alone with my pretty aunt, who now seemed doubly desirable to me, excited me greatly. But I was still feeling the effects of my session with the estate manager's wife and had to remind myself that rushing things could well and truly compromise my plans.

After looking round the library Marguerite went over to the table and stood there sifting through what was on it. She could well have made some interesting discoveries. Lying on top of the table was Volume O of the Encyclopaedia, with a bookmark inserted at the page on Onanism, while in the margin opposite the word I had pencilled in a question mark. I heard her close the book, and then the Anatomical Atlas, over certain of whose plates she had lingered for some considerable time. So when I entered the library I was scarcely surprised to find her with cheeks a bright shade of red.

I pretended not to notice her embarrassment and said to her gently: 'I bet you get bored too sometimes, auntie dear. The priest who used to live here once had some jolly interesting books about human nature. Why not take a few into our room?'

I picked up a couple – *Marriage Unveiled* and *Love And Marriage* – and slipped them into her pocket. As she was making rather a show of reluctance, I added: 'Just between you and me, of course, that's understood. We're not children any more, are we, auntie?' And I suddenly flung my arms round her and gave her a smacking kiss.

Her hair was done in a becoming chignon and her exposed nape was delicious. Attractive chignons and lovely necks have always stirred me profoundly, so I planted upon my aunt's nape a series of resounding kisses which utterly intoxicated me. But as for Marguerite, she was still under the influence of her recent confession. She pushed me away, though not harshly, and after a last glance towards my room, beat a retreat, carrying off the books in her pocket.

In the course of the afternoon I heard the cleric leave with the ladies. I decided to look for Berthe and ask her why she found it necessary to feign illness in order to get out of confession. But it wasn't like that. She was in bed and really did seem ill. So my visit cheered her up.

My innate sense of mischief was soon aroused. But when I sought to fondle her under the covers, she turned away and said: 'No Roger, I've had a period since the day before yesterday... you know very well... and I'm too ashamed...'

'Ah!' I said, 'your menses, eh. So you're no longer a little girl, but a woman. I've become a man, too, Berthe,' I added proudly. Unbuttoning, I showed her my pubic hair and bared prick. 'And what's more, I've done it too, you know! But I can't tell you with whom.'

'You've done it?' Berthe queried. 'Done what, though?'

I therefore explained coitus to my attentive sister.

'And you know what, papa and mama do it too, all the time.'

'You're joking! That's disgusting.'

Her tone implied precisely the opposite, so I added: 'Why disgusting? Why were two sexes created then, Berthe? You've no idea how nice it feels, and it's so much better than doing it on one's own.'

'Yes, it always did seem better when Kate wanked me than when I did it myself. As for the day before yesterday, well, I thought I was in heaven! Then Kate told me: "Now that you've come, Berthe, watch out, you'll soon be getting your period." That very day I had stomach-ache and suddenly something wet ran down my thighs. I was really scared when I saw it was blood! Kate started laughing and went to find Mama, who came and had a look at me and said: "Get into bed, Berthe, you'll have this for three or four days every month. You'll need to change your night-gown when the bleeding stops. Don't wash yourself before then or else it won't stop. You won't be wearing little-girl dresses any

157

more." I'm going to have long dresses like Mama and Aunt,' Berthe concluded with some pride.

'Come on, Berthe, let's do it.' And I kissed and hugged her close.

'Don't hurt my breasts,' said Berthe. 'I'm very sensitive there now.' But she made no objection to my opening her night-gown to see her little breasts in their primal bloom. They were a pair of tiny hillocks that put me in mind of a young Psyche or Hebe: they already had the classical form, showed no sign of sagging and tautened into tiny, twin pink sweetmeats on offer.

I murmured soothing words to her and she willingly let me fondle, and even suck, her breasts. That excited her, however, and after a few token protests she let me see her cunt, but only by dint of my first rolling up her bloodstained nightgown.

She was already far hairier than I. A little watery blood was trickling along her thighs; it was certainly none too appetising, yet I was too excited to be put off. She was keeping her thighs closed tight, but my finger soon located her clitoris. Her thighs opened under the pressure from my hand. Finally, I was able to put my finger into her wet cunt, but not very far, for she contracted. I pressed against her hymen, in the middle of which there was already a little hole. Berthe uttered a brief cry of pain and tensed up again.

Very excited now, I rapidly undressed, lifted my shirt and climbed on top of my sister, intending to force a member growing harder by the second into her cunt. Berthe protested in an undertone, began crying and gave a sudden moan when I was well and truly inside her vagina. But the momentary pain seemed to turn into pleasure. Her cheeks were hot and flushed, her pretty eyes sparkling and her mouth half open. She clasped me tight and responded vigorously to my thrusts. Before I had finished, the nectar started flowing from her cunt. Her eyes half closed and fluttered nervously. She cried out loudly, but her cries were of pleasure: 'Roger, ah! ah! ah! Ro-o-oger – I... I... aah!' She was completely beside herself. I had deflowered my sister.

Because of my morning fuck, and my acute excitation, I had not yet come. The sight of my sister's climactic delight aroused me still further and I increased my rhythm. But I suddenly felt something warm in Berthe's cunt. I withdrew, and a bloody ooze – a mixture of my sperm, the blood from the torn hymen and the menstruation – flowed out. We were both very scared. My member was covered in blood, which was also plastered to my hair and balls.

Our fright knew no bounds, however, when we heard a voice behind us declare: 'My, my! Aren't the young folk having a nice conversation!' Kate was standing right beside us.

She had forgotten something and had been sent back to fetch it. So absorbed were we in our pursuits that we had not heard her climb the stairs, but apparently she'd spied on us for some time from outside before opening the door quietly and tiptoeing in during Berthe's voluptuous climax.

Her mischievous features reflected the state of excitement induced by what she had seen and heard. Berthe and I were so taken aback that for a while we did not even think to cover ourselves or rearrange our clothes. Kate had ample time to view Berthe's copious bleeding and the shrinking of my prick, which fear had caused to detumesce.

'When doing this sort of thing,' Kate laughed, 'be sure to lock the door!' And she went across and bolted it. 'Berthe, your mother forgot to tell you not to do it during periods. But I know how it is,' she added, laughing heartily, 'that's just when you most want to. I suggest you put a dry cloth between your legs, Berthe, and stay quietly in bed. But this shirt shouldn't go in with the dirty washing, Roger, unless you've started having periods too.'

Then I saw that my shirt was bloodstained. Kate poured some water into a basin and brought it over to me.

'Luckily it'll come out easily,' she said. 'Get up, Roger, and I'll give you a wash.' I stood up facing her so she could soak my shirt, but this proved awkward. She then promptly whisked off the shirt and thus I was stark naked in front of the two girls. She washed the shirt mockingly, but then said: 'Well come here!' in a more serious tone, and washed me with the sponge. On contact, my prick gently began to rise. Kate remarked: 'Oh, you naughty cock, sneaking into Berthe's cunt!' And she gave it some playful little slaps. All of a sudden she grabbed me, left-handed, pushed me to my knees and spanked me as hard as she could. I started shouting. Berthe was doubled up with laughter. My buttocks were smarting, but I felt an even more powerful excitement than before.

When I was ten my mother, because of some misdemeanour of mine, once wedged me between her thighs, pulled down my breeches and gave my juvenile buttocks an almighty thrashing. After the initial pain wore off, however, a feeling of sensual pleasure stayed with me for the rest of that day.

When Kate noticed that my prick was once again highly presentable, she burst out laughing. 'Oh! Oh! what a big crankshaft Roger's got! Let's turn the starter, let's turn the handle!' She took my prick in her hand, squeezed it then unsheathed its head. I could bear this no longer. I grasped hold of her tits, while she put up a show of resistance. Then I slid my hand beneath her skirts. She was not wearing knickers. I seized her apricot. She tried to pull away but I had her by the short-hairs. My left arm encircled her arse. I knelt down and sank the thumb of my right hand into her warm cunt, working it in and out. She was enjoying this, there was no denying it, and she resisted only half-heartedly. As she staggered close to Berthe's bed, the latter, so as not to appear embarrassed in front of Kate, assisted me by throwing her arms round Kate's neck and pulling her down towards the bed.

Kate lost her head and fell upon the bed. I lifted her dress and exposed her cunt. Her pubic hair was red, not as thick as I'd thought from what Berthe had informed me, but quite long and moist with sweat. Her skin was milky white and smooth as satin. Her white thighs were pleasantly rounded and were becomingly sheathed in black stockings, which also enclosed a pair of firm round calves. I flung myself upon her, thrust my prick between her thighs, gently penetrated her cunt. But I withdrew almost immediately. I had nothing to brace my feet against. The position was too uncomfortable.

But Kate, who was now on heat, jumped up, pushed me into the chair next to the bed and threw herself on top of me. Before I had time to get my bearings, my member was imprisoned in her cunt. I felt her long pubic hairs against my belly. She was rocking to and fro and holding my shoulders. With every stroke her big lips nipped my balls.

She removed her thin percale blouse of her own accord and told me to play with her bubbies because, she said, it felt so good. Her tits were naturally better developed than Berthe's and harder though far smaller than those of the estate manager's wife. They were white as her thighs and belly and tipped by two big red peaks, surrounded by more yellowish areolae on which there were some tiny hairs.

Kate, very excited, was nearing her crisis. The violence of her movements was such that my prick twice slithered out of her cunt and she hurt me getting it back inside, although she herself seemed to be deriving considerable pleasure in so doing. I was coming in a poor second, while she was already yelling in ecstatic tones: 'Now... now... now... it's coming!... Ah! Oh! Oh! my God... your prick's so ni-iice.' At that she came and I was aware of the increased wetness of her cunt. In the final throes of her ecstasy, the sensitive chambermaid bit my shoulder. Feeling her boiling ejaculation, I sensed that my own eruption was approaching.

Kate had rapidly regained her selfcontrol: 'Roger, your dick's getting hotter and hotter, you're going to shoot off now.' And she stood up abruptly, her right hand seized my prick dripping with her juices and began frigging it violently. While doing so she said: 'Or else I might get pregnant.'

I too had risen to my feet. Kate pulled me against her with her left arm; I sucked her nipples. I must have parted my legs. Stark naked as I was in front of the two absorbed girls, my loins were shaken by sudden spasms. Suddenly my sperm spurted. Berthe watched the ejaculation intently and gazed curiously at the white liquid which had fallen onto the bed.

Kate the sophisticate, while I was discharging, had been tickling my arsehole, encouraging me with: 'There, my Roger, you're coming nicely, there you go... that's it.'

My orgasm had been indescribable. After it I fell back into the chair. Kate behaved as though nothing had happened. She tidied everything, wiped my prick with her handkerchief, rebuttoned her blouse, picked up her basket and remarked to us with her customary jauntiness: 'Thank God it all turned out like this! Be sensible, now. You, Berthe, stay in bed and rest, and Roger, you go back down now!'

She left and I returned to my room, after I'd dressed and given Berthe a kiss.

Chapter Eight

The day's events had left me absolutely exhausted. My sole desire was to rest.

When I awoke the next morning I was lying on my back, a position which generally gave me an erection. Soon afterwards I heard footsteps. I wanted to play a joke on the estate manager's wife. I raised my nightshirt, flung back the covers and pretended to be fast asleep. But instead of the estate manager's wife it was her sister-in-law. She was a woman of about thirty-five, the age when women are at their most sensual.

In her younger days she had been a chambermaid. Having married an elderly valet who'd a tidy sum in savings, she now lived with her husband and three children (a son and two daughters aged ten, eleven and thirteen) in her estate manager brother's quarters.

Madame Muller was neither beautiful nor ugly. Tall and slim, she had a dark complexion and jet-black hair to match her eyes. She seemed intelligent and well worth a fuck. It was perfectly obvious that she'd seen more than one knob in her life. In which case, she might just as well see mine too – and so I didn't budge.

Madame Muller placed the coffee on the bedside table, then, catching sight of my weapon at the ready, she was momentarily smitten with astonishment. But she was a resolute woman, free of false modesty. She observed me intently for a few seconds, with some pleasure at that. Then she coughed to awaken me, and as I stretched in such a way as to bring my prick even more insolently to the fore, she approached the bed, glanced at me briefly and pulled the covers back over me, saying as she did so: 'Your coffee, Monsieur Roger.'

I opened my eyes and said good morning, along with a compliment on how well she was looking, etc. Then I suddenly jumped out of bed, grasped her, and assured her she was the most beautiful woman in the whole Château. She resisted feebly and when I slid my hand beneath her skirts I laid hold of a very hairy mound. Then I plunged my finger into her cunt. It was dry, as with all sensual women, but my finger soon had it moist. Her clitoris was very hard.

'Here, what's the matter with you? Stop it! If my husband knew what you were doing – !'

'Monsieur Muller's in the chapel.'

'Yes, he goes and prays there all day long... But stop that now, you're hurting... My sister-in-law might come in... she's waiting for me... That's enough! I'll come back tonight... now's not the right time... My husband's leaving today for two or three days in town.'

With that promise she took her leave. That evening, after a good dinner, I brought back to my room some wine, ham and dessert. The Château was soon asleep. At long last my door opened. Madame Muller came in and my heart began pounding. I embraced her, a French kiss which her tongue reciprocated. I speedily undressed and showed her my prick in fine fettle.

'Don't get too excited,' she said, 'it'd be wasting it, otherwise.'

She bolted the door. I gripped her mound and found it slightly swollen, the clitoris hard. I undressed her down to her petticoat and raised it aloft. One would have thought her on the thin side when dressed, but she wasn't at all. She was actually well-upholstered, with black pubic hair which climbed up as far as her navel.

She must have washed, for her cunt was odourless. Then I stripped her naked and was surprised at the firmness of her bubbies. They were not very large and the nipples were surrounded by sparse light brown hairs. Cupping and raising her

164

breasts I saw that under them she also had short, fine black hairs. Her armpits were likewise covered with tufts of hair thick as a man's. Examining her, I marvelled at her arse, whose unusually jutting buttocks were tight-set. Fine black hair also ran from the top to the base of her spine. This luxuriant fleece stiffened me still further. I flung aside my nightshirt, of course, and flung myself astride the beautiful female whose writhing movements made my prick slap against her belly.

We were in such a position that we could see ourselves full-length in the mirror. I led her towards the bed, where she sat down, saying: 'I know you want to see all of me.' She lifted her legs and displayed her hairy cunt as far as the arsehole. I immediately began quim-tonguing and took my time about it. The lips became swollen. When I sought to insert my prick, she laughed and said: 'Not like that, get on the bed.'

I politely suggested we used the informal *tu* when addressing one another, and got onto the bed. She climbed on top of me and I had her whole beautiful body there before me. She told me to play with her tits. Then she grasped my cock, grazed it a bit across her cunt, inside which she begged me not to come, and suddenly stuffed my prick in right up to the balls. She was riding me with such ardour that it was almost painful. She discharged during this time; I felt the full heat of her cunt and heard her groan as her eyes rolled back into her head.

I was also getting near, and when she realised this she briskly uncoupled. 'Hold it, my sweet,' she said in a voice still trembling with sensuality, 'I know something else you'll like which won't make me pregnant.'

She turned round. Her buttocks now faced me. She bent down and took my prick in her mouth. I followed her lead, my tongue sliding into her cunt. I lapped the female fluid, which tasted of raw egg. The play of her tongue against my glans became more insistent, and with one hand she tickled my balls and arse as with the other she squeezed my prick.

So great was the pleasure that my whole body went rigid. She rammed my prick as deep as possible into her mouth. Her most secret parts stared me full in the face. I seized her thighs and plunged my tongue up her arsehole. I took leave of my senses and came into her mouth.

When I recovered from my short-lived rapture she was lying beside me and had pulled the covers back over us. She was caressing me, thanking me for the pleasure I'd given her, and asking me if it had been as pleasurable for me. I had to admit that that position had made me come even more copiously than straight-forward coitus. Then I asked her why she hadn't let me come in her cunt, since she was married.

'Precisely because of that,' she said. 'My husband is impotent and would realise the moment I deceived him. Ah, God, what I have to endure from him!'

I urged her to tell me all about it. She told me her husband could only get an erection if she caned him until his buttocks bled. She, too, had to let him beat her, though only with his hand, and now she was so used to it that it gave her more pleasure than pain. She was also obliged to piss, even to shit, in front of her husband, since he wanted to see everything! Which was why he got particularly randy when she had her periods.

After she had whacked him fifty or maybe even a hundred times, she'd have to be quick about shoving his half-turgid member up her cunt or else he'd soon go limp, except when she licked his arse or let him lick between her toes. On those occasions he kept good and hard but all these sordid goings-on were extremely disagreeable.

'And what's more,' she ended up, 'the old so and so spends most of his time in church.'

This surprising tale had revived my dick's rude vigour. Madame Muller hastened the resurrection by tickling my balls. She got me to lie in between her legs, and then turned over on her side. Her legs scissored my buttocks and we were facing each other, both lying on our sides. This was a most enjoyable posture for it allowed us to lie closely entwined. I could suck her tits, too.

I was holding her swollen cunt, its actual passage now narrowed by our recent love bout. We each had a finger up the other's arsehole. I let my prick glide into her cunt, and began rocking, as before. I sucked her tits. My finger was moving about in her arse, which I could feel throbbing. She started crying out as she again came. She had grasped my balls from behind so tightly that she hurt me and I begged her to let go of me.

After caressing me gently she turned face down on the bed to show off her arse. I made her kneel with arse thrust out, then spat into her arsehole and sank my prick into it, bumming a ride without difficulty. At each stroke I felt my balls thwack her cunt.

She kept saying how good it felt. I was able to fondle her hairy cunt with one hand and palp her breasts with the other. Just as I was about to discharge I started to withdraw, but she contracted her sphincter around my knob and I let fly right inside her arsehole. She had never done it that way before, and she told me that although to begin with it had hurt her a bit, she had really enjoyed it by the end. Feeling my prick stiffen in her arse had stirred her lust and she'd come again at the same time as myself.

'But that's enough for today,' she decided, smiling.

I'd had enough too. I offered her some dessert, but she invited me for a quick liqueur in her room. After that I went back to bed.

Chapter Nine

One day my mother decided that all the maids should sleep on the top floor of the Château, under the eaves. They began to move their belongings up there, with a view to sleeping there that very night. I watched them move.

Just as one of them, mattress under arm, was slowly climbing the last flight of stairs, I got behind her and hoisted her petticoats. First I grabbed a firm pair of buttocks, pressing these against me while sinking my thumb into her moist cunt. She uttered no cry, but on turning and recognising me she smiled as if flattered by my gallantry. It was Ursula, the brunette. I led her up to the top floor and embraced her.

She seemed to take it very well, this first kiss, and indeed initiated the second. So I grasped her tits and soon had the firm, brown-tipped hemispheres nuzzling at my right palm. A swift sinistral lunge under her light, short skirt and her hirsute hillock was there to hand.

She squeezed her thighs tighter and leaned forward slightly. I took a tittie in my mouth and sucked at it while my finger toyed with her clitoris, which I found to be in an acutely stimulated state. Soon my hand slipped between her thighs and one, two, three digits penetrated her cunt.

She tried to get away, but I pushed her against the wall. I felt her whole body tremble beneath her flimsy clothing. I pulled out my prick quick and thrust it into her cunt. The position was awkward and since the young girl was tall and strong, I'd never have been able to fuck her if she hadn't pulled her weight. So I fucked her standing up.

She must have been hot for it, because she came quickly enough. I, too, was on the point of coming, due to the very fatiguing position, but we heard noise from the nearby rooms and Ursula uncoupled. But the noise promptly died away. I then showed her my dark red prick dripping with her discharge. She looked at it keenly, for as she said, it was the first time she'd ever seen a city swell's prick.

'Right, let's see you then,' I said to her. She modestly complied. I raised her skirt, enabling myself to see her very lissom legs and, between her firm thighs, an impressive black thatch. Thank God she was not wearing knickers like city ladies do, all airs and graces when you fiddle with their cunts, despite enjoying it as much if not more than the peasant girls. I stepped back, still holding up her skirt and blouse, then moved in close again and let my hands rove over her belly and thighs.

After this I buried my nose in her cunt which smelt of egg – due to her recent discharge – and of piss. When my tongue reached her clitoris she started laughing and let her skirt fall back into place. But I held on tight and continued drooling all over her body underneath her dress, getting yet another hard-on. Since the noise had recommenced, however, Ursula pulled away again, this time for good. It was my cue to leave, but as she turned to go I lifted her skirts one last time from behind and bared her truly superb and admirably firm arse.

'Just a bit more, Ursula,' I said, holding her fast by her blouse. I kissed her buttocks, handled them, parted her cheeks to smell her arsehole, which exuded no odour of shit, but only of sweat. She finally broke free once and for all, remarking that she didn't understand how a gentleman like myself could get any pleasure from sniffing the smellier places on a peasant girl's body.

That evening at dinner I softly asked Berthe if I could fuck her. She said no. I went upstairs to see whether I might find some opportunity of doing what I so greatly desired. But I found none.

My bed was already turned down. I undressed and lay naked upon my stomach, spreading a handkerchief underneath me. Hugging my pillow I thus polluted myself, thinking about my aunt, my sister, and all the arses and cunts with which I was acquainted. Then I rested awhile, before beginning this process of masturbation again. At the very moment I felt the sperm coming, I heard a voice from behind the door say: 'Monsieur Roger, are you asleep already? I've brought the water.'

I rose, put on my dressing gown and opened up. It was a kitchenmaid called Hélène. As soon as she was inside I bolted the door. My desire was so great that my member was bobbing to and fro like a pendulum. I immediately grabbed the attractive and rather well-dressed peasant girl by her firm bum and big tits, and planted on the latter a pair of smacking kisses. She took all this in good part, but when I got to her cunt, she told me, blushing: 'It's my period'; which was just my luck. I was stiff as a Carmelite and she was looking at my prick quite obligingly. She played about with it very nicely too. At least I could divert myself with her tits. I opened her camisole and the two tits popped into my hands. They resembled their owner in that they were freckled all over, but were otherwise irreproachable.

I gave her no peace until, albeit somewhat reluctantly, she let me see her arse and her cunt, whose curly red hairs were stuck together with blood. I pushed her onto a chair and let her place my prick between her knockers. This proved highly practical: it disappeared between the breasts, whose resilient fleshy folds were most agreeable. It would have been better had the divide been wetter. I told her so. She spat on my prick and between her tits, then stuck my prick back in there and squeezed her breasts together tight. The knob could be seen peeping out at the top while the balls dangled below the bosom.

Then I began swaying back and forth, whispering sweet nothings to her and at the same time patting her face or playing with the curls on her nape. There followed a powerful discharge, which she watched attentively, since this way was as novel for her as for me.

Having had my fill, I made her a present of a silk scarf, which she very cheerfully accepted, apologising for her condition. She added that the girls who worked with her in the kitchen went to bed late, but that in the morning she usually slept on later than the others, who rose very early to go milking. If I were to go up there, I'd find myself even better satisfied.

Her information pleased me enormously. The next morning I fabricated a pretext – installing a dovecote below the eaves – in order to get an opportunity to climb up to the maids' garrets. But my project was frustrated for I was constantly being interrupted. I did once catch Berthe in the lavatory, and Kate once also, and got a look at their cunts. But because of the inclement weather my mother and my aunt were chatting away assiduously and neither Berthe nor Kate dared do more than grope my prick in passing.

To kill time more pleasantly I'd made a hole in the lavatory partition; the lavatory itself was simply a hole in the ground. And I could spend the afternoon watching all the girls and ladies shit, piss and fart. I could study bums, arseholes and cunts in all their splendour and I saw that they varied only in hair colour and plumpness. I was persuaded of the truth of that statement attributed to a farm lad allowed by a countess to fuck her. When they asked him about it, he replied: 'The blouse was finer, but apart from that, it was just like with other women.'

I was thus able to see all the arses and cunts in the Château, and the spectacle afforded by even those women I'd already fucked was a constant source of pleasure to me.

Meanwhile I'd presented Ursula with a pretty headscarf, for it was no fault of hers that I hadn't been able to fuck her completely. The other girls had noticed it, and all turned thoroughly winsome where I was concerned. No fools they, for they soon realised it was very nice to be fucked and to receive a present into the bargain. That's what one of them told me, early one morning whose profound stillness was broken only by the muffled sounds of activity in the stables.

I had gone upstairs and found one unbolted door which led into two bedrooms. There was an atmosphere inside this room of mingled odours emanating from the maidservants' bodies. Their clothes were hanging from the wall or draped over the foot of the bed. At first these odours were distinctly disagreeable, but as soon as one got used to them they became exciting rather than oppressive. This was the veritable *odor di femina*: the perfume that brings you a stand.

The beds, made up in the old-fashioned style, were double. All were empty save one, in which a girl lay snoring loudly. She was lying on her side, facing the wall. One of her feet was on the wooden bedstead and thus her arse was even more prominently exposed to my view, since she was sleeping in the nude.

Her coarse shift lay on a nearby wooden chair, along with her other clothes. The sleeper's name was Babette and she had not the slightest idea she was being appraised from head to toe. Her skin could have been softer; her build was stocky rather than slim.

I brought my face close to her arse and sniffed the pervasive aroma of her sweat. Her arsehole still retained some traces of her last crap. Above it her closed cleft, crowned by chestnut hairs, was clearly visible. I gently tickled her buttocks and cunt. As soon as I inserted a finger therein, she gave a start and turned over. I could contemplate her from the front. Her fleece was curly and smelt strongly of piss, which fact I noted when sticking my nose into it. I should add that these maids washed their cunts only on Sundays. Anyhow, there are plenty of fine ladies who have no time to do so more often. Yet this odour excited me and I already had a hard.

I bolted the door and stripped off. Then I spread her thighs. She half opened her eyes. 'Babette,' I said, thrusting three fingers into her cunt, 'you're my little sweetheart. See how stiff I am!'

She stirred, pointed towards the other room, and said: 'Ursula's

173

in there, too.'

'That doesn't matter, we've got time to do it before she wakes up. Look, this is for you.' And I gave her a little imitation ring I'd bought from a pedlar. Then without another word I knelt between her legs which she willingly parted. I let her play with my prick and balls while I tickled her cunt. When she was nicely ripe I drove it in up to the balls, raised her buttocks and tickled her arsehole. She clasped my neck and together we plunged into a voluptuous frenzy culminating, after a brief engagement, in a violent discharge by both parties.

During the action, she had perspired profusely and her healthy young country woman's odour made me hopeful of shooting off a second salvo. I thought of shagging her doggy-fashion. But she was scared of getting pregnant. Besides, she had to get up because this was Ursula's day for having a lie-in. I had quite forgotten Ursula and Babette laughed a lot when I told her I wouldn't mind waking Ursula up.

While Babette wiped off her cunt with her nightgown, I went through into the other room where Ursula was still fast asleep. She, too, was nude, but with the covers pulled up to her bosom. She was on her back, both arms tucked under her head so that the thick black bushes in her oxters were on view. Her pretty tits stood out all the better for the position of her arms, on either side of which the long, thick curls of her hair tumbled charmingly down. This whole picture was a delight. A pity she was only a peasant: yet I fail to understand how a man can prefer a society lady's affected charms to the natural beauty of a peasant girl.

Her immaculately clean shift was beside her. I sniffed it and marvelled at the healthful odour with which it was impregnated. Very gently I drew back the covers and admired her nakedness. I stood for a moment in amazement at the superb sight of her well-proportioned limbs and that richly furred motte whose black hairs ranged from her nether lips to her thighs. She awoke while I was kissing her breasts. She was startled and at first covered her pubis with one hand. Then, recognising me, she gave me a pleasant smile.

Just then Babette appeared in the doorway and said: 'Stay in bed Ursula, I'll do your work.' And with that she left.

I kissed Ursula until she grew thoroughly randy. I asked her to get up and made her walk around the room, so I could properly admire her lovely figure from all angles and from top to toe. Then I clasped her very tightly in my arms and we stood there, entwined like this, for some time. I planted both my hands upon her buttocks and pulled her belly against mine. She could feel the stiffness of my prick and her short-hairs tickled my balls. She liked this game. She put her arms around my neck; her chest pressed into mine. I tugged at her armpit tufts. She became wildly excited. I put my hand into her cunt, which was wet and distended. Her clitoris was absolutely hard.

We got into bed. I had her kneel and thrust her arse into the air. I inspected her arsehole feverishly. Her cunt, crowned by black hairs, was partly open. I delightedly observed her rather red cleft, then rubbed my glans against the lips. She enjoyed that. She assisted my movements: I slid in smoothly to the hilt, then pulled out, and so on back and forth until I felt on the brink of coming.

She was coming like a madwoman, her thoroughly distended cunt tightly gripping my member. I poked it right in, all the way, forced myself against her arsehole, palped her tits and jigged about like a lunatic. I was quite out of control. She was groaning at every thrust. With one hand I squeezed her tits, with the other I tickled her clitoris. We came simultaneously. I listened to my prick twitch and click inside her sodden cunt. We lay there as though dead.

When I withdrew I was still erect. She was ashamed, because she'd never let herself be fucked that way before. What she'd most enjoyed had been the slap of my balls against the lower part of her cunt. I was not yet done and would have liked to spend longer with this lovely, wholesome girl. Had it been possible, I would have married her.

She told me she had to go downstairs. She put on her blouse and I helped her dress. She was smiling in a friendly way. I looked her over once more before leaving. I promised to buy her a fine keepsake and she agreed to come and spend the night with me soon.

Chapter Ten

The Château was still asleep when I went downstairs again and back to bed. My mother woke me up when she brought my breakfast. She informed me that I should have to go to the station the next day to meet my father, who was arriving with my eldest sister, Elise.

My mother was in an extremely good mood, but not so Berthe, annoyed at her very pretty sister's impending arrival. She told me Elise was having a flirtation with the son of one of our father's business associates, and that the young man would probably marry her after doing his military service. She also told me that numerous things she had not understood before were now abundantly clear to her. Obviously Kate and Elise must have played tribades together over a long period of time, and once they had even remained closeted alone in the bathroom for a whole hour.

The next day it pleased me to note that my mother was having a bath in anticipation of my father's visit. At the station, when the train arrived, I was amazed to see that my sister Elise had turned into a charming young woman. She had pretty little feet and a pair of elegant shoes on them, and she moved with such graceful undulations that I became quite jealous of her Frédéric. I had decided that every female member of my circle should form part of my harem, and I now strengthened that resolve.

My jealousy increased when I saw that my father had brought along a friend, M. Franck, an elderly bachelor with expectations where my aunt was concerned. The introductions were cordial. My sister was as surprised by my development as I was by hers, and our embrace was more than just sisterly or brotherly.

We hadn't counted on M. Franck, and since the carriage only seated two, I said that papa and M. Franck should use it while Elise and I would walk home. My sister agreed. The road back was very pretty.

The conversation soon took an interesting turn. My sister was very flattered by the compliments I paid her beauty. When she inquired about Berthe, I said she had had her first period and was now nubile. She looked at me in astonishment.

'She stays locked in the bathroom with Kate just as long as you used to,' I added. Then, watching her closely, I went on: 'They sleep in the same room too, if you follow me.'

My sister blushed deeply but remained silent.

'No need to be embarrassed, Elise,' I said amicably. 'I'm not a little boy any more. Anyhow, you must have noticed when we were given baths together in our younger days that my prick's no worse than your Frédéric's.'

'Why, Roger!'

'We've got hair between our legs now and we know there's something better than getting your finger wet or tossing off.'

She flushed bright scarlet, her bosom was heaving, but she was at a loss for words. She glanced round abruptly to see whether anyone was looking at us, and asked: 'Is it true, Roger, that before going into the army young men have to strip naked and let themselves be examined? I overheard mama and aunt saying something about that, and at the hotel it was being discussed too.'

'Frédéric, my future brother-in-law, could have told you about all that. Certainly they have to. They get examined like a bride on her wedding night. But they don't have erections because they're scared. Frédéric can't have had a hard-on either.'

'Oh come on now!... But they must feel ashamed... Is it in public? Can women see that?'

'Unfortunately not,' I said seriously. 'But in front of you, Elise,

I wouldn't be embarrassed.' I kissed her warmly. We were in a small wood near the Château. 'Do you imagine,' I added, 'that there's a bride in the whole world who won't have to strip naked on her wedding night and be duly inspected by her husband? He strips, too, in any case.'

'But it's not the same for a man.'

'Why not? If I were to strip in front of you, you'd see everything: my short-hairs, my prick stiffening, my balls; but with you I'd only be able to see your hair, your cunt would stay hidden. Do you have a lot of hair there, Elise?'

'Oh, look at those lovely strawberries, Roger,' said Elise.

I helped her pick some. We went deeper into the wood. Erect as a rutting stag, I embraced her.

'What's that over there?' she asked.

'A hunting lodge. It belongs to us, I have the key.' The lodge was surrounded by a thick copse.

'Wait for me, Roger. I'll just be a moment. Make sure nobody's coming.' She went behind the lodge. I heard her pissing. I looked. She was squatting, leaning forward slightly with her legs apart, and she was holding her skirts high enough for her pretty calves to be visible. The lace edges of her knickers hung beneath her knees. The jet was spurting between her legs. When it stopped, I was going to retire discreetly, but she stayed crouching. She hoisted her skirts above her loins and pulled down her knickers. The cleft of her arse was exposed, along with her firm, plump, spotless buttocks. The result of her effort was a thin sausage which emerged from her arsehole, waved about briefly then twirled onto the ground. A little juice followed, then she pissed a bit more. In this way I distinctly discerned the stream squirting from hairs that were chestnut-coloured and relatively thick. When she had finished, she searched for paper but found none. I then appeared and gave her some. 'Here, Elise.'

For a moment she looked angry.

'Don't be embarrassed,' I said to her. 'I want to go, too!' I pulled

179

out my prick and, although I was still hard, began pissing. I remembered the manservant and pissed so high that my sister had to laugh. She'd used the paper. We heard voices. She became apprehensive and I pushed her inside the lodge and closed the door after us. We looked out through a crack. A farm worker and a serving maid approached, fondling each other. He threw her to the ground, climbed atop her, pulled out his prick, raised her skirts and they went at it grunting like animals.

I'd put an arm round Elise and pressed her close to me. Her scented breath warmed my cheeks. Her bosom was heaving deeply as we watched this spectacle in silence. I pulled out my prick and placed it in her hot satin-smooth hand. The couple went away. I couldn't resist and seized Elise. Despite her resistance, I soon flung aside knickers and jacket. My hand toyed with her short-hairs. Her thighs were locked tight but I could feel her clitoris hard.

'No, Roger, that's going too far! Have you no shame? I'll scream!'

'If you scream they'll hear in the Château... Nobody'll know. Primitive man did the same thing.'

'But we aren't primitives, Roger.'

'Elise, what if we were on a desert island...!' I managed to get a finger inside.

'If my Frédéric ever found out!'

'He won't know. Come on, my sweet.' I sat on a chair and pulled my sister on top of me. When she felt the massive prick against her cunt she gave up struggling. She was no longer a virgin and admitted having done it once with her Frédéric. Her cunt was narrow, very hot and pleasantly wet.

She returned my kisses. I opened her blouse and coaxed out both her tits which bobbed about as I was sucking them. My arms clasped her firm, jutting lower spheres, that magnificent pair of buttocks. She began coming very violently. We came together. Afterwards we vowed each other to silence. We looked ourselves over in leisurely fashion, then went back to the Château.

Chapter Eleven

At table everyone was very animated. My father was being attentive to mama. M. Franck was proving highly solicitous towards my aunt. I conversed with my sisters. My room had been allocated to the guest. I was to sleep on the same floor as the women, in Elise's room, while she shared Berthe's, along with Kate.

When everybody was asleep I peeped into my sisters' room. Berthe was sleeping but Elise was not there. I saw a light, hid myself and caught sight of Elise and my aunt in their nightgowns, spying through a crack in my parents' door. The sounds of loud smacks on a bare arse were audible. Then my father raised his voice: 'Now drop your nightgown, Anna... How lovely you are with your black thatch.' Kisses and whispers. 'March, Anna. Forward march!... Halt!... Arms up in the air... What a lot of hair under your arms... Look how stiff I am, Anna, take it... Present arms!... Shoulder arms... come here!'

'Now Charles, don't get too excited... you're hurting me... you've looked at me enough. I'm embarrassed, letting you stare at my behind.'

'Relax, my child... Get on the bed... feet in the air... higher... there... my treasure...'

The bed could be heard creaking.

'Coming, Anna?'

'Soon, Charles!'

'Anna!... I'm coming!...'

'Oh, that's it, that's good... Charles... Ah! Ah!'

Kate's voice was audible on the stairs. Elise heard her and slipped back into their room. My aunt dashed into hers without shutting the door. She re-emerged. My parents had put out their light. I went into my aunt's room. As she came back in, she started in fright. I told her everything. She relit the light. I kissed her without saying a word. I felt the splendid curves of her lovely body. She was trembling. I groped beneath her nightgown for her cunt. She struggled. I comforted her. 'Let's be husband and wife, darling, pretty Marguerite!'

My finger played with her clitoris. She gave way. I uncovered her snowy mounds, those beautiful white breasts. I pushed her towards the bed. She began sobbing. I suggested our eloping to get married. That made her laugh. I bared my prick. She was, too, excited by the champagne she had drunk. She blew out the candle. I put my prick into her pretty hand, then I tickled her pussy; the pleasure was too great, she writhed around, her clitoris swelled. I put a finger up her cunt and sucked her tits. Then I lifted her nightdress, pressed her against me mouth to mouth and with forceful thrusts worked my stiff dick into her virginal cleft.

A solitary, fleeting cry preceded the paroxysm which almost immediately overwhelmed her. This was a woman now ablaze with passion and she abandoned herself to the voluptuous crisis. A brief bout, but one whose sensations were infinite, brought both of us to the brink of the most frenzied ecstasy, and it was with the most brutal lunges that I spurted the vital essence into her womb.

The pleasure had been too great, I still stayed stiff. I caressed her then relit the candle. She hid her face in the pillows; her modesty had returned, but I drew back the covers to view the body of a veritable Venus. There was a slight trace of blood on her cunt hairs, mingled with our come. I wiped her clean with my handkerchief, turned her over, stroked her back and buttocks and stuck my tongue up her arsehole.

Then I mounted her, my head buried in her perfumed hair. My arms encircled her body, raising her slightly, and I plunged my cock once again into her moist cleft. A long bout ensued which had us sweating from every pore. She was first to come, screaming with pleasure like a madwoman. My discharge followed, almost painful in its ecstasy. That was enough; we separated.

Several weeks passed, bringing pleasures of one sort or another. M. Franck was courting my aunt more and more assiduously. One day, Elise and my aunt entered my room in tears. They were pregnant. But neither dared, in the other's presence, name me as the guilty party. My mind was soon made up.

'Elise, marry Frédéric, and aunt, you marry M. Franck. I'll give both of you away.'

The morning of the following day, my door opened and Ursula entered. She, too, was pregnant. I told her to marry the estate manager's cousin, who'd been making eyes at her, and I promised to stand as godfather to her child. Then I undressed her and licked at her cunt and arse. After that I doused myself with *eau de cologne* and made her lick my arse. That aroused me enormously. I fucked her with such gusto in my thrusts that her hair fluttered all over the bed.

Soon there were three weddings. All turned out for the amorous best and I took turns sleeping with the women of my harem. Each knew what I was up to with the others, and they all got on well.

Ursula soon gave birth to a boy, and Elise and my aunt in due course had girls. On the very same day I became godfather to Ursula's little Roger, to Elise's baby Louise, and to my aunt's little girl Anna – all children of the same father, though this they will never know.

I hope to have many more and thereby fulfil a patriotic duty, that of increasing my country's population.

[1] *comme une mouche, une mouche assassine.* Archaic phrase for a black silk patch, usually worn on the face, as a fashion accessory. I have tried to approximate Apollinaire's pun on *mouche* (fly).

[2] The book's French title is *Les Onze Mille Verges ou Les Amours d'Un Hospodar. Verge* can mean both 'rod' and 'penis'. English slang allows for both these meanings in my title, but loses an important punning French reference to *les onze mille **vierges.*** These 11,000 virgins, followers of St. Ursula, a Cornish princess, were supposedly journeying through Europe after a visit to Rome when massacred by the Huns at Cologne, circa. 4th or 5th century AD. Their number is, as Rev. E. Brewer pointed out, 'purely fabulous'. Another commentator, Attwater, is harsher still in his 1965 *Dictionary Of Saints*: 'this pious romance was preposterously elaborated through the mistakes of imaginative visionaries'. All of which must have delighted Apollinaire, who refers to the legend and his own title finally and neatly in the book's last words, with the rhymed quatrain that serves as Mony's epitaph. As for *Hospodar*, Flaubert's entry for the word in his *Dictionnaire Des Idées Reçues* was: 'Sounds well in a remark on the Near East question.' Given Mony's pretensions and prejudices in the novel, and Apollinaire's tortuous and somewhat tongue-in-cheek explanation of the term, a satirical view of Mony as Byronic (or Sadeian) aristocrat and sardonic dandy is implicit throughout.

[3] *l'automédon* (sic). Automedon in Greek mythology was charioteer to Achilles, then to Pyrrhus, his name synonymous with dexterity. Less obscure and more current around 1907, if not now, is Jehu (II. Kings IX, 20), who lent his name to any coachman, especially to one driving at a rapid pace.

[4] Eponym of a proud, even absurdly meticulous maître d'hôtel. Vatel, a veritable prima donna of cuisine, stabbed himself to death over a fish shortage that disrupted his projected menu for Louis XIV. In two letters to her daughter (24 & 26 April 1671) Mme de Sévigné graphically describes this tragic (yet also, in Apollinaire's view, perhaps grimly comical) event.

[5] Alphonse Allais (1854-1905). Great French humorous writer, practical joker and café wit. Friend of Cros, Verlaine, Satie, Apollinaire

et al, and, like Jarry, abbreviated his – still highly productive – life via absinthe.

[6] Apollinaire's (italicized) 'signature'. One well known journalist of the time wrote an account of a drunken Apollinaire at a literary dinner ordering Apollinaris (*'C'est mon eau'*...): this led to preparations for a – finally unfought – duel!

[7] 'Estelle Ronange' is supposedly and scurrilously based on the famous actress Marguérite Moréno, widow of Marcel Schwob (1867-1905), a writer Apollinaire knew and admired. Like himself, Schwob was widely read and travelled, and had been something of an impresario and enthusiast for the arts, as well as a fount of arcane, archaic and curious reference and knowledge. *Le Français* here refers to the *Comédie Française*.

[8]   Long-established (Napoleonic) statute of rules for *Comédie Française* actors concerning work 'outside' the state theatre company.

[9]   This – typically ironic – nuptial invocation, a rhyming sonnet (ABAB/BABA/CDD/CEE), simultaneously borrows as its last line one from Act IV of Corneille's *Le Cid*, and manages a punning joke ('obscure clarity') on M. Claretie, Administrator-General of the *Comédie*, with whom Moréno (see Note 7) frequently quarrelled. 'Avinain' remains obscure.

[10] Two minimalist scatological sonnets, rhymed respectively ABAB/ABAB/CDD/CEE and ABAB/ABAB/CDC/DEE. Omphale: Queen of Lydia, who bought Hercules from Mercury as a slave. Thereafter their amorous enslavement became mutual. Pyramus & Thisbe: Apollinaire's variation on Shakespeare's *A Midsummer Night's Dream*, with the unfortunate lovers here somewhat bolder and indeed achieving gratification.

[11] *comme une grive dans les vignes*. Literally, 'like a thrush in the vines'. Conflation of *soûl comme une grive* = dead drunk, and *être dans les vignes* = being drunk. For this now rather obscure if not archaic piece of slang I have substituted an equivalent phrase in use at the turn of the century.

[12] Valley of Jehoshaphat. Jehoshaphat was the fourth King of Judah (circa. 874-850 BC). The valley mentioned in Joel III.2.12. is a play on his name (i.e. 'the Lord has judged') but it is not clear whether Joel there designates geography – the Wadi Kidron – or is dramatizing some

future judgement.

[13] I have retained Apollinaire's versions (oddly enough, given his own ancestry, these are French rather than Slavic spellings) of historical and political personages. In 1903 the corrupt rulers of Serbia, King Alexander and Queen Draga, were assassinated by the 'Black Hand' secret society. Here and in the Russo-Japanese War material later in the novel, Apollinaire combines real people and events with fictional inventions.

[14] French journalist contemporary of Apollinaire, surname spelt 'Barre'. The playful practice of only slightly changing a real person's name, or merely transposing various letters, occurs later in this novel (see Note 22; also Part 9, where 'Genmolay' is Apollinaire's friend Jean Mollet) and was later adopted by writers Apollinaire influenced, such as Boris Vian.

[15] Mony's usual pretentious and haughty tone is here satirized by Apollinaire, via the sort of sonorous inventions (*Pétropolitains... suspections...*) his recently deceased friend Jarry would have enjoyed.

[16] Again, Apollinaire at his most Rabelaisian-Jarryesque. A punning disquisition on both balls and linguistic roots. Knowledge of English and Latin, as well as of French, is required to make the learned joke clear: *tête*-testa-testis-testiculus; mentula-mens-mental, etc.

[17] Leucas or Leucadia: Ionian island (also known as St. Maura) off one of whose promontories, near Apollo's temple, lovers would ritually leap. Sappho, when spurned by Phaon, the boatman of Lesbos for whom she cherished a passion, is said to have flung herself into the sea from there.

[18] Ovid (43 BC-17 AD) was banished in his 50th year, and at the height of his fame, by the Emperor Augustus. Conjecture has it (as Apollinaire suggests here) that the reason for the poet's sudden exile was his knowledge of the Emperor's incestuous relationship with his daughter Julia. The five books of *Tristia*, according to Lemprière, 'contain much elegance and softness of expression' whereas *Epistles From Pontus* 'are the language of an abject and pusillanimous flatterer'.

[19] 'Daddy's Delights' does not sound quite as convincing a name for 'the modish dive of Port Arthur'; I have let the French stand.

[20] Title (or line) of song italicized and in English. The spelling of cosey is not necessarily an eccentricity or misprint. Partridge's great

Dictionary Of Slang notes that in pre-1909 London slums the word referred to 'a small, hilarious public-house, where singing, dancing, drinking, etc., goes on at all hours'.

[21] Russian for 'God save the Tsar'.

[22] 'Adolphe Terré' and 'Tristan de Vinaigre' were Adolphe Retté and Tancrède de Visan, symbolist poetasters. (see Note 14)

[23] Apollinaire puts in 'the rustling forests' phrase, one of Retté's book titles, to cause further annoyance, and moves to more slapstick parody, bringing in (possibly via 'the dark wood' and its association with Dante) an excreting Virgil.

[24] *Bitchlamar*. Probably an Apollinairean invention.

[25] *The Forty-Seven Rônin*. These were leaderless Samurai avenging their executed master in 1703. The Kabuki play based on this true 18th century story was later translated by Masefield. The next title, *The Beautiful Siguenai*, has proved untraceable; the Shigenoi, however, were a noble 12th century family. The Taiko cycle is well known, if not *Taiko* as given here. *The Great Thief*, mentioned by Kilyemu later in her story, has also proved untraceable.

[26] Daibutsu of Kamakura: The huge bronze Buddha at Kamakura, once the capital of Nippon (Japan). This seated statue is 50 ft. high, 97 ft. in circumference; its face 8 ft. long and the thumbs several feet round.

[27] *kellnerine*. Apollinaire is presumably thinking of the German or Dutch words for a waiter/waitress. He uses this term several times.

[28] Salpêtrière. Home in Paris for aged and mentally sick women; originally for ex-prostitutes. Mony's inimitable and insulting response to the Slav exiles and anarchists centred in Paris, whose bombing exploits had been a source of outrage up to the time of writing (1907).

[29] Boccaccio's collection of 100 tales, *The Decameron* (1353) was represented as having been told over ten days by ten storytellers, during the plague at Florence in 1348.

[30] the Trinity Ame-no-Minakanushi-no-Kami... Izanagi and Izanami... Ama-Terasu...: Shinto deities. The supreme celestial divinity, and the others more or less as Apollinaire describes them, with the sun goddess Amaterasu-o-mikami having been born from the left eye of Izanagi. The *koto* mentioned here is the traditional flat lute, but a *sio* is apparently an Apollinairean invention.

[31] This poem, rhymed ABBA/ACCA/A/DADA/, whose first two verses appear in an earlier Apollinaire MS., seems to be included for no very good reason except (as the narrator of this story-within-the-story implies) as a critical comment on, and acknowledgement of, youthful Symbolist influences. The poem may also be referring (verse 3) to Apollinaire's mother, Angélique. *Neniae* are classical funeral dirges or, more simply, sad or lamenting songs.

[32] Arcola, Italy. Scene of Napoleon's victory over the Austrians, 1796. Bara, the drummer boy killed in this battle, became legendary, and there were many sculptures and paintings of him during the 19th century by David and others.

[33] During the Russo-Japanese War, the Japanese invaded Manchuria in February 1904, captured Port Arthur on 2 January 1905, and won Mukden on 9 March 1905. A Japanese naval victory followed in the Tsushima Straits that May, and a peace treaty was signed at Portsmouth, USA on 23 August 1905. The victorious Japanese lost 75,000 dead, the Russians 120,000.

Also available in this series:

PHILOSOPHY IN THE BOUDOIR
The Marquis de Sade
(Velvet 1)

In the boudoir of a sequestered château, a young virgin is ruthlessly schooled in evil. Indoctrinated by her amoral tutors in the ways of sexual perversion, fornication, murder, incest, atheism and wanton self-gratification, she takes part with growing abandon in a series of violent erotic orgies which culminates with the flagellation and torture of her own mother – her final act of liberation.

Philosophy In The Boudoir is the most concise representative text out of all the Marquis De Sade's works, containing his notorious doctrine of *libertinage* expounded in full, coupled with liberal doses of unbridled eroticism, cruelty and violent sexuality. The renegade philosophies put forward here would later rank amongst the main cornerstones of André Breton's Surrealist manifesto.

This seminal text is presented in a new, modern and authentic translation by Meredith X, herself a former dominatrix.

ISBN 1 871592 09 7 £4.95

THE SHE DEVILS
Pierre Loüys
(Velvet 2)

A mother and her three daughters...sharing their inexhaustible sexual favours between the same young man, each other, and anyone else who enters their web of depravity. From a chance encounter on the stairway with a voluptuous young girl, the narrator is drawn to become the plaything of four rapacious females, experiencing them all in various combinations of increasingly wild debauchery, until they one day vanish as mysteriously as they had appeared.

Described by Susan Sontag as one of the few works of the erotic imagination to deserve true literary status, *The She Devils (Trois Filles De Leur Mère)* remains Pierre Loüys' most intense, claustrophobic work; a study of sexual obsession unsurpassed in its explicit depictions of carnal excess, unbridled lust and limitless perversity.

ISBN 1 871592 51 8 £4.95

THE PLEASURE CHATEAU
Jeremy Reed
(Velvet 3)

The story of Leanda, mistress of an opulent château, who tirelessly indulges her compulsion for sexual extremes, entertaining deviants, transsexuals and freaks in pursuit of the ultimate erotic experience. She is finally transported to a zone where sex transcends death, and existence becomes a never-ending orgy of the senses. The book also includes *Tales Of The Midget*, astonishing erotic adventures as related by Leanda's dwarf raconteur versed in decades of debauch.

In the decadent and erotic tradition of De Sade, Sacher-Masoch and Apollinaire, *The Pleasure Château* is a tour-de-force of perverse sexual delights; a careering midnight excursion through the labyrinths of a young girl's most secret desires.

Jeremy Reed, hailed as one of the greatest poets of his generation, has turned his exquisite imagination to producing this masterpiece of gothic erotica, his tribute to the undying flame of human sexuality.

ISBN 1 871592 52 6 £4.95

Watch out for these forthcoming titles:

THE WHIP ANGELS
Anonymous
(Velvet 5)

Victoria's journal reveals her darkest secrets, her induction into a bizarre yet increasingly addictive sexual underground at the hands of her immoral, incestuous guardians.

Behind the façade of everyday life seethes black leather mayhem, constantly threatening a voluptuous eruption of demonic angels from timeless torture zones, a midnight twist heralded by the bullwhip's crack and the bittersweet swipe of the cat.

Blazing with erotic excess and incandescent cruelty, *The Whip Angels* is a feast of dominance and submission, of corrupted innocence and tainted love. In the tradition of *The Story Of O* and *The Image*, this modern classic was written by an anonymous French authoress fully versed in the ways of whipcord and the dark delirium of those in both physical and spiritual bondage.

ISBN 1 871592 53 4

£4.95

HOUSE OF PAIN
Pan Pantziarka
(Velvet 6)

When a young streetwalker is picked up by an enigmatic older woman, she finds herself launched on an odyssey of pleasure and pain beyond measure.

Lost in a night world, thrown to the lusts of her anonymous captors, she must submit to their increasingly bizarre rituals of pain and degradation in order to embrace salvation.

House Of Pain is scorched earth erotica, an unprecedented glimpse of living Hell, the torments and raptures of a young woman abandoned to the throes of rage, violence and cruelty which feed the sexual impulse. Churches, hospitals, courtrooms, all become mere facets of the same unyielding edifice, a bedlam of desire and flesh in flame beneath the cold black sun of her own unlimited yearnings.

ISBN 1 871592 57 7

£4.95

Also forthcoming:

Available from good bookshops, or direct from the publishers @ £5.50 including postage & packing. Credit cards accepted.
A catalogue of other publications is available on request.
Creation Books (Dept V), 83 Clerkenwell Road, London EC1, UK.
Tel: 0171-430-9878 Fax: 0171-242-5527.